LETTERS from RACHEL

N. L. WESTAWAY

Original Cover Marlene photo by Daiga Ellaby
Cover designed by Beach House Press

This book is a work of fiction. Names, characters, places, and incidents either are products of the author's imagination or are used fictitiously. Any resemblance to actual persons, living or dead, events, or locales is entirely coincidental.

N. L. Westaway
Visit my website at www.NLWestaway.com
ISBN: 978-1-7339442-8-1
Printed in the United States of America

First Publication: December 2020 Beach House Press

Letters from Rachel

This book is dedicated to my mother, who loved a good mystery.

Thank you to Brenda, Eddie, and Lawrence for your assistance with my research regarding the first responder, medical, police procedural, and the clinical psychology knowledge necessary in order for me to accurately portray the characters in this novel.
Thank you to Cathy my friend and editor, for painstakingly going through the pages of this latest novel. Your support and kindness had been much appreciated during this difficult time in 2020, and your encouragement is something I will be forever grateful for.
To my hubby, I am grateful to you for your never-ending love, your reassurance that my writing is never a waste of time, and your constant words of reassurance and support with any project I choose to take on. There is no one I would rather share a beach house with than you! xo

"The most loving parents and relatives commit murder with smiles on their faces. They force us to destroy the person we really are: a subtle kind of murder."
— *Jim Morrison*

Chapter 1

"Yes father," Rachel said despite the fresh injury. How many times in her 18 years had she said those words, when what she desperately wanted was to scream, *"No!"*

With graduation only a week away, Rachel still had not been able to give her father an answer about what she would be studying at *his* college. He had used this as an excuse to beat her again, but this would be the last time she would be subjected to his violence. He had given her until the end of the week, and it was Friday now and the last day of high school. Though, her plan hadn't been to give him an answer today, instead she planned to go to the police finally, before the school day started, and report the abuse.

At the police station, officer Robert Thompson had taken her statement, then asked that she wait in the lobby area.

Out in the waiting area, Rachel watched a door open and a young man strolled out of what she'd assumed was the chief's office, it being the only closed-door space in the station other than the one marked *interview room*, of the ones she could see, anyway. Even the holding cell was the open-air kind, like a giant cage with just a short bench inside.

The young man walking towards her was very tall, tall dark and handsome she mused. She didn't recognize him, but then she didn't get out much and didn't really know anyone in town and definitely not any of the men, not if her parents had anything to say about it.

"Fill out the forms, Jamie — get your life in order," said a deep commanding voice from within the office and just before the door to it was slammed shut. The sound vertebrated through the precinct, and Rachel watched as the other visible officers scrambled around trying to look busy. The handsome young *Jamie* passed by then and turned his head to smile at her.

She smiled back and watched as he turned away and headed out through the main doors.

"You can go now," the officer said from behind the desk, grabbing her attention. "We'll send an officer to the house to investigate. Don't worry, we'll make sure things are taken care of." He gave her a nod.

She nodded back, grabbed up her school bag, and without a word, she headed out of the station and off to school.

Officer Bradly Stinson pulled up and parked the cruiser alongside the front yard of Professor Michael Rampton's home. The house was an older colonial-style home, its most obvious attribute being the symmetry. It was rectangular in shape, not the traditional two storeys, but a bungalow with the door located in the center with the same number of windows reflected on either side.

At the front door, Officer Stinson gave two swift knocks and then waited.

A woman who looked old enough to be the complainant's grandmother promptly answered the door. "Yes, hello officer —

how can I help you?" the woman said, holding the door open a mere half-foot.

"Gooday, ma'am, is Professor Rampton available?" Officer Stinson straightened up and puffed out his chest.

"No—he's at the college. Is there something I can help you with?" She glanced behind her as if trying to keep something out of view.

"Does a Rachel Rampton live here? There's been a complaint, ma'am." Officer Stinson tried to see through the door and past the woman's head.

She opened the door wider then. "Come in officer. What has that hellish child done now?" she said with a huff and an eye-roll. "I'm almost embarrassed to claim she's my daughter."

"Well," Officer Stinson said, recognizing now as he passed through the doorway into the front hall, that he was speaking to Rachel's mother—not the grandmother. She'd had Rachel late in life, he figured. Her hair was short and wavy, mousy brown but mostly grey, even her eyes were a dull brown, and she wore no makeup or jewelry, not even a wedding ring. Her clothes consisted of a shift-style dress in a muted brown colour over which was a long grey apron. She carried an off-white dishtowel in her right hand, and she smelled strongly of pine sol and bleach, he noted. "The complaint was made by her—not about her," he corrected, rubbing a finger under his nose, irritated by the cleaning product smells.

"What?" she asked, changing her tone to that of a much younger more virtuous woman than her appearance presented. "A complaint about what?"

"Not *what*, ma'am—who," he stated, glancing around the entry hall. The space was exceptionally neat and tidy, as was the living room, the only room he could see from where he stood. He wondered now what it was she thought she was hiding from him.

"Who?" she asked, shutting the door with the dish toweled hand. Her other hand she brought to her throat, running it up and down her neck to her collarbone.

"Her father, ma'am," he said, sliding his thumb through the side loop in his tactical belt.

"My husband—are you serious?" she questioned, turning to stack the already tidy mail on the sideboard next to the empty coat rack.

"Yes, ma'am." He sniffed.

"Muriel please—call me Muriel," she said checking her watch.

"Mrs. Rampton, when is your husband expected home?" he asked, growing restless. He did not care for the back and forth dialog, in fact he wasn't exactly interested in investigating some prominent professor from his hometown.

Muriel cleared her throat, then checked her watch again. Changing her stance to a much stiffer posture, she said, "Our daughter has always been a bit of a storyteller. Usually just trying to get her father's attention in one way or another." She checked her watch a third time. "Always misbehaving," she added firmly, as if closing her point.

"These are some serious allegations, ma'am," he stated, shifting his position to get a better look into the living room. "Can you please have your husband—Mr.—Professor Rampton, come down to the station as soon as possible?" He squinted, trying to see into the room at the end of the hall but the door was partially shut.

"I'm sure this is all a misunderstanding—I apologize Officerrr...," she started, searching for his name badge.

"Stinson," he added for her, turning back towards the front door.

"Officer Stinson—yes, I'm sorry you had to come all the way out here over another one of Rachel's lies." She cleared her throat again. "My husband and I will address this with her—once she is home from school," she added, reaching over to open the front door.

"Please have your husband call the station—to follow up," Officer Stinson requested, doing his job yet assuming he'd wasted his time and his lunch hour driving out there for some teenager's parental issues, rebellion, whatever. "Gooday, ma'am," he said, exiting the home.

The door closed behind him.

"What a hag," he mumbled to himself, relieved to be out of there, strolling eagerly down the front walk to the police cruiser.

At 3:30 p.m. Rachel opened the door to her home and walked to her bedroom, feeling safe for the first time in her life, despite knowing she would have to deal with her mother over this. Her father would be sitting in that jail cell by now and asking for his one phone call. He would call his lawyer first before calling her mother, that was for sure. She smiled at the thought then dropped her school bag on the corner of her bed and glanced around the room.

Her bedroom was where she spent most of her time if she wasn't studying at the library or expected in the kitchen to help her mother. The room had been painted white and had dulled with age, and it had light grey wall-to-wall carpet. There were no posters or artwork on the wall as you might find in a typical teenager's room. They had not allowed Rachel to put anything on the walls. The only furniture was a twin bed, a dresser that held her clothes, and next to the only window was a child-size desk and chair that they expected her to do her homework at. The room itself, was sized for a young child, not a grown teenager.

There was a closet, but it held only her winter coat and boots, plus a second set of bedding of which she was responsible for washing each week. She was given a standard amount of laundry soap to do so, but she was never given any fabric softener, so her bedding had become worn and paper-like and was neither cool in the summer nor warm in the winter. The bed was just a mattress and box-spring on a metal frame, and had a single unimpressive pillow covered by a dark grey comforter that she had had as long as she could remember. It too, had not weathered the laundry and was now scratchy and had lost its thermal density to provide any warmth. She had no mirror in the room, and she was given very little time to bathe each day and get ready for school.

The house itself had only two official bedrooms now, the third bedroom, one much larger than hers, the one between hers and the master, had been converted into her father's office. The office was where he spent most of his time when not at the college, and where he most often chose to conduct her beatings. He had decorated in the style of a pretentious scholar, with a large decorative dark wood desk and a plump dark leather chair. The walls had been lined with bookshelves matching the style of the desk and were filled with hardcover and leather-bound books she realized when she had opened some, he had never read. But she was done with that office, she was done with him, and she was done with high school now too. All that was left to her senior year, was the ceremonial part of her graduation and then she would be free.

She laughed then and spun herself in a circle, arms outstretched like a ballerina. On a second spin, her mother's silhouette came into view of the bedroom's doorway, and Rachel stopped.

There was a substantial purple bruise that stretched the length of her mother's face from temple to jaw, and the lower right side of her lip was swollen and still leaked blood. Large hand-shaped red compression marks encircled her neck, and the expression she gave Rachel was one of loathing.

"You think I look bad," her mother said, dabbing her lower lip with a dishrag. "This is what I got—for telling your father what you did. For not being able to control my ungrateful daughter." She winced and dabbed her lip again. "Wait until he's done with you," she added indignant, but was abruptly shoved aside out of the way then, replaced in the doorway by Rachel's father.

Rachel in her shock, still noticed that he had taken his regular work dress shirt off already, as was par for the course with his beatings. *"Wouldn't want to make a mess of my good shirt now — would we,"* the memory of his voice echoed in her head. He still wore his suit pants, and like usual, he unbuckled his leather belt and drew it through the loops to end in a sharp *snap* as the strap pulled loose.

"Your mother had a visitor today," her father said, taking a step into her room. "Apparently, you made a visit to the police… had a report written up… a complaint… about me." He wrapped the buckle end of the belt around his left hand, then holding the end of the length in his other, he snapped it straight. Snapping the belt a second time, the sound resonated within the small room, as he took another step closer.

Rachel stepped back, her legs meeting the edge of her bed, the comforter's fabric scratching the back of them. Behind her father stood her mother again in the doorway. Rachel watched as her mother reached for the doorknob, grabbed ahold of it, and then yanked the door shut.

"How dare you embarrass me—how dare you bring disgrace upon my name," her father said, seizing her attention again. He was a well-known, well-respected literary professor at Cambridge College here in Massachusetts, but his level of condescension was as if it were the famed Cambridge University in the UK. And other than his reputation, school and books were the only things he ever cared about. She had tried to please him by getting good grades, exceptional grades in fact, getting extra credits, even pushing herself to graduate with honors. But over the last few years, the beatings had often still been about her grades, the occasional *A-* being enough to evoke embarrassment upon his name—or so he had claimed. She had never seen him this angry before, although she had never done anything like this before either. She never disobeyed him, never went out, never had a friend over, she kept to her room, only ever coming out to help her mother with meals or to go to school or the library. Before this, she had never been brave enough to tell someone what was really going on in their home, well, other than her mother.

"Your mother has enough to deal with regarding the care of this home, tending to the needs of this family, to be bothered in the middle of the day—interrupting her chores, to deal with a police officer at the door," her father said through gritted teeth, his words thundering out, spit forming at the corners of his mouth.

She glanced down, focusing on the tips of his expensive loafers. Her *mother* was basically a slave to her father, and it was not a marriage in the traditional sense Rachel had come to realize, not with the proclivities he had had for her when she'd been a child. From the age of five, she been abused by him, sexually abused. Never penetration, but he had made her do things to him, disgusting vile things that had given her enough nightmares to last ten childhoods. However, when she had reached puberty, the sexual abuse had stopped only to change to regular beatings instead, as if it had sickened him to witness her mature into womanhood. These beatings were always accompanied by the name calling, *whore*, *slut*, *tramp*, and often proceeded by the 'f' word to give them more weight, and all despite the fact that she was still a virgin, had never had a boyfriend, or even a friend for that matter. When she had turned sixteen, she had finally had the courage to tell her mother. Although, her mother had not believed her, and in her denial, she had turned a blind eye. Better *me* than her, she had probably rationalized.

"Look at me—you little bitch," he ordered, snapping the belt in her direction.

Rachel knew by his malevolent expression that this would be the cruelest beating of all beatings, and she was not free… she would not be… she was nothing and no one—not even her mother cared what happened to her. She drew in a deep breath as her father took one last step forward and snapped the belt again.

When it was over, Rachel's father leaned down to her and whispered in her ear. "I'll give you 20 minutes to think about what you've done." His breath smelled of onions and some kind of liquor. A drop of his sweat hit her cheek before he lifted his head away, though she still kept her eyes closed. "Then get your ass up off the floor and go help your mother in the kitchen with dinner," she heard him say before hearing the door shut.

She had let him beat her, she had not fought it, hadn't even called out in pain like she had typically done before. This time she had not wanted to give him the satisfaction of her resisting, of hearing her cries. He had hit her harder for it, used the buckle end of the belt and had cut her upper thigh open, but she had gone somewhere else, had let her mind escape during each brutal blow. She had not been free… but she was now, and she had a new plan.

This evidence, these welts and bruises now forming across her arms and legs, she figured would show them she had been telling the truth. He never hit her face, she was lucky for that she guessed, but that was more to keep hidden what he had been doing, and you couldn't hide a black eye. They lived out of town and a ways from where her father taught, so any bruises or injuries that her mother may suffer would never be seen since no one really ever came to the house. But if the police came back now, they would see what he had done to her mother, not that Rachel cared, but it would be more evidence in *her* favor.

Rachel cautiously turned on her side. The dress she had worn today had been torn off leaving her in her underwear and tank top, and she chose to leave the ruined garment where it had been thrown. With little time to spare, she forced herself up on her knees, then reached beneath her bed for the jeans, sweatshirt, and boots she had stashed there. Standing then with a wince and a hushed moan, she leaned on her dresser and opened the drawer that held her underwear.

Next to her folded undershirts was a box of maxi-pads, which she grabbed, opened, then dug into to get the money she had hidden there. It was the safest spot. Her father would never touch it, and her mother in menopause now, wouldn't need them, so it had been the ideal place to hide her earnings.

She had been permitted the option to get a job at the library to have money to buy books—and only books, other purchases had not been allowed. Her father had plenty of money, but he never spent a dime on anyone but himself. She already spent a significant amount of time at the library studying so it seemed the perfect place for her to work, her father had said, and her mother felt it would keep her out of trouble and out of her way. They hadn't known it, but Rachel had worked a heck of a lot more than they knew, and she had still managed to keep up with her excellent grades.

She liked her boss, a typical librarian, exactly how you would picture one, and she appreciated Rachel's love for books. She had even paid her under the table for the extra shifts she had worked, mainly because she did not like Rachel's father, didn't like that he limited how often she could work or even what she was allowed to spend the money on. "He was an arrogant misogynist twit, who knew little about books despite his teaching literature.

He liked the sound of his own voice," her boss had said to Rachel. She had attended his class and had taken an instant dislike to him, but she suffered through the class for her love of literature and library studies. She had told Rachel that he talked about great works, though he had never written anything, and had only read the classics, and just the ones that those in his field felt were worthy of reading. She knew Rachel hated him, hadn't known why, but Rachel knew she had felt a kinship in the disdain.

Leaning to the side, Rachel snatched up her school bag and opened it to empty out her graduation ceremony paperwork and the yearbook she had been given, onto the floor. She did not want or need either of these things. Then she tucked the wad of cash into the front zippered pocket. She followed next with placing the jeans and sweatshirt in the main compartment. Continuing, she pulled several pairs of underpants, some undershirts, and socks—all white cotton of course, from the open drawer, tossing one of each to change into onto the bed, transferring the rest into the filling bag. She didn't own any bras—not one, her mother had never bought her one, as it had been an order from her father. All her clothes had been chosen for her, dresses mostly—which she had liked actually, were purchased two sizes too big to hide any marks from the beatings, and to hide her womanly body, another demand from her father. Her favorite dress, a dark green cotton long-sleeved one covered in yellow and white petaled flowers, the one she'd actually had a chance to grow into, had been thrown out by her mother—or so her mother had thought. Rachel had rescued it from the trash bin, washed it with the rest of her things and then had hidden it away with other treasures she had collected over the years. And today, today was the day she would wear that dress. She loved the colours and the soft cotton fabric, and she especially liked how it complemented her green eyes and long dark russet hair, hair that if the sun caught it just right, it shown gold ribbons throughout its dark wavy tresses.

Reaching now behind the dresser, she slid out a plain brown paper bag, the one she had been keeping the dress in. She changed out of her undergarments and into the set she had laid on the bed. She pulled the dress from the bag and then gingerly, she pulled the dress over her head. With a grin, she yanked on her socks and then stepped her feet into her new black combat-style boots and laced them up.

Before gathering up the last of her things and adding them to the bag, she used some of the gauze bandages she had hidden to seal up the cut on her leg. With only minutes before her name would be yelled from down the hall, Rachel swiftly secured back her hair into a long braid. She packed her remaining items into the knapsack and zipped it, then lifted it up over her right shoulder... and then she climbed out her bedroom window.

Out of habit, she had left her bike near the side of the house out of view of the driveway. The bike was a one speed, front brake, piece of crap, that she'd had to fix any issues with it herself, but it had been the only way for her to get to and from school and to the library other than walking the 5 to 7 miles, depending on where she was going. She had even ridden it in the winter when the roads were clear, because otherwise she had had to walk.

She slid both arms through the straps of the knapsack, then eased herself on to the seat. With a creak from the bike and one painful push, she was off pedaling towards town as fast as her wounded legs could take her.

Arriving at the police station, she rested her rust covered bike against the steps to the main entrance. She tidied the bandage on her leg, smoothed her hair back of any strands that had come loose, and then swung her bag over one shoulder before climbing the steps.

Opening the door, Rachel spotted Officer Thompson, the one she had originally given her complaint to. "You'll have to believe me now," she spouted, pushing up her sleeves to show the welts. As she was showing her legs and pointing out the bandage, another officer walked in through the front doors to overhear what she had been saying.

The two officers could not have been more different. Officer Thompson was average height and very thin, with jet black hair cut in a military crewcut style. He had a large nose and thin lips. This other officer was short and chubby, with barely-there carrot-top red hair and a shiny pink face to match his shiny pink balding head.

"I know all about your attention getting antics young lady— we don't have time to play these games with you," pinky-pig face said. "I spoke to your mother at the house and then again over the phone—and your father too." He stepped even closer, and she saw that his neck was covered in acne scars. He smelled like cheap cologne and sweaty body odor. He had almost certainly been bullied in school for his appearance and probably why he felt the need to be the bully now.

"My mother lied," Rachel said, through clenched teeth. She had had enough of intimidation in her short life. "Officer Stinson," she said, reading his name tag. "When my father heard what she had done, letting a police officer into the house, he beat her too. She has a huge bruise on her face, a fat lip, and choke marks on her neck. Go check, see for yourself, I'm not lying."

"Your mother told us you often hurt yourself to get others in trouble," Officer Stinson said, tossing the accusation out and sliding his thumbs between his waistband and the bulging heft of his belly, gripping his belt.

The door to the police chief's office suddenly flung open and a tall middle-aged man with salt 'n pepper hair stormed out.

"Chief," Officer Stinson said, stepping back from Rachel, clearly intimidated by the man, the years of receiving bulling himself even more evident.

"What the hell is going on out here, Thompson?" the Chief said, addressing the other officer and ignoring Stinson.

"Miss Rampton is back, Sir. She claims she's been beaten again."

"Claims?" Rachel shot back. "What do you call this?" She stretched out her arms to show the welts, then bent to lift the bottom of her dress. She felt a hand on her shoulder, and she spun, flinging an arm out and smacking the person accidently on the side of the face.

"Whoa—ouch," Jamie said, rubbing the side of his face.

"Oh-my-gawd—I'm so sorry," Rachel said, reaching and gently removing his hand from his face to see if she had caused any damage.

In the middle of the commotion both junior officers began talking, explaining things at the same time.

"Stinson—get in my office!" the Chief said, shouting the order. "Jamie, wait here until I'm done. You too have some explaining to do." The senior officer turned away then and strode swiftly back into his office.

Officer Stinson immediately followed, scurrying as if he were a *bad* dog, while Officer Thompson fiddled with a stack of papers behind the front desk, ignoring Jamie and Rachel as they stood silently in the front lobby.

"Let's sit," Jamie said, extending an arm towards the chairs.

Calming now, Rachel nodded and then sat in the chair closest to the main doors.

"I'm Jamie," he said, smiling and extending a hand.

"Rachel," she said back, shaking his hand. His smile was warm and his eyes, dark brown, were kind, unlike those of his father's.

"What happened to you?" Jamie asked, still holding her hand, turning it to examine the big purple wounds on her arm.

She let go of his hand and took in a deep breath. "My father," she said, letting her breath out in a sigh.

"Your father did this?" Jamie asked, his anger escalating.

"Yes," she said, drawing back the hem of her dress to reveal more of her injuries. "But they don't believe me. I told them this morning—they said they'd take care of things, but they didn't, and when I got home from school... well... I just can't take it anymore." She pulled the sleeves of her dress down, covering the bruises as a sense of defeat flooded her.

The door to the Chief's office opened then and both the Chief and Officer Stinson walked out. Then Officer Stinson walked past them without saying a word, to exit out the main doors.

"Jamie," the Chief called, pointing a thumb over his shoulder towards the open door of his office.

Jamie glanced at Rachel.

"And you—Miss Rampton, you need to get on home, and stop all this foolishness with giving your parents a hard time— and wasting our time."

"Sir, I don't think she should...," Jamie started.

"Don't speak unless spoken to, son," the Chief said, cutting him off. "You don't know this girl."

"I know she's hurt," Jamie said, in defense of her. "She shouldn't have to go back home to her father—she's clearly been abused."

"I just spoke to her mother on the phone—she explained everything to me. The girl is a runabout, neglects her schoolwork, acts up at home, and is always disobeying her father."

Rachel's blood pressure pulsed in her ears and her adrenaline rose as she stood. "She's a lying bitch—and my father is an abusive sick bastard," she screamed. Her composure crumbling, she turned away from the Chief, this horrible man who had glared at her with judging eyes, judging her over lies her mother had spewed. Then without another thought, she grabbed her knapsack off the adjacent chair and darted for the exit, pushing open the main door. The weight of the door swung back hard on its hinges as she raced through it and down the stairs.

"Rachel, wait!" Jamie called after her.

Outside Rachel fussed with her bike, the tire had gone flat while she had been inside. She gave the tire a swift kick just as she heard Jamie call her name again.

At her side, he said, "I believe you." She looked up, and he was smiling at her again. "My dad is an asshole."

"Yes, he is," she agreed, feeling a smile tug at the corners of her mouth. A strand of hair blew loose from her braid then.

"Where are you going," Jamie asked, seizing the loose strand, and tucking it behind her ear.

She glanced down at her bike and shook her head. "Nowhere by the looks of it," she said, kicking the tire of her bike again. "Flat tire." Where could she go now? Her rickety old bike had a flat, not that she could head out of Dodge on a bicycle, anyway. She hadn't thought that far ahead, all she knew was that she had to get out—get away. But now what? "Piece of shit," she added, letting go of the bike and letting it drop to the ground.

"I can give you a ride," Jamie offered, pointing over to an old motorbike parked at the corner of the parking lot. "But we'd better go before my father comes out looking for me."

Rachel glanced up at the main doors, then back over at the motorbike.

"C'mon, I'll take you to my favorite place," Jamie said, his warm smile stretching across his face. "Gimme your bag."

"Okay," Rachel said, giving in and handing him her knapsack. What did she have to lose? Then the two of them darted over to the motorbike to make their getaway.

Jamie handed her his leather motorcycle jacket, then took a second helmet from one of the side bags. "Put these on," he told her. He buckled up his own helmet, put her knapsack on backwards with the big pouch in front on his chest, then he straddled the bike and quickly started the engine. "Climb on," he said, over the roar of the motorbike.

Rachel gathered up her dress, pulling the back hem through her legs to the front and then sat astride the seat behind him. As the bike kicked forward, Rachel wrapped her arms around Jamie's midsection and then they were off.

Rachel had no idea where they were going, but anywhere was better than home, better than the police station. As the bike sped along, she clung to her rescuer for both safety and comfort. She had never been this close to a boy, but Jamie wasn't a boy, he was a man, and for the first time in her life, she actually felt *safe*. She didn't know what she was going to do next, but what she did know, was that right now this is where she wanted to be... with him.

At the end of a long country road and as the bike slowed, an old worn red barn came into view. "This is my grandfather's property," Jamie said over his shoulder, bringing the bike to a stop. "The barn isn't used much these days. There's a new one closer to the house. He pointed to a house way across the field. She could see a more modern structure adjacent to a modest white farmhouse. "But I love coming out here to this one," he said, helping her off the bike and handing back her bag. "It's a great place to get away to... away from my father... for some quiet, just to think, ya know."

Rachel nodded. She knew what he meant. The library was like that for her. She had loved the quiet and the opportunity to be out from under her parents. "Thank you," she said, "for getting me out of there."

"Ya, well, I wasn't interested in sticking around there either," Jamie admitted. "My dad said we needed to talk, but he pretty much just yells."

Rachel nodded again. She knew what that was like too, though she knew worse than that. However, she appreciated that he was sharing with her, trying to relate on some level. She didn't get to talk with many people, none really, maybe her boss at the library occasionally, but the library was a quiet space, not a chatting space, and she was enjoying this, enjoying his company, enjoying him. And she had never had a friend like him before.

She watched as Jamie slid the large barn-door aside and then pushed his motorbike into the open space of the structure. "Coming?" he asked, motioning for her to come in. Swinging her bag over her shoulder, she followed him in.

Rachel glanced around the barn. It looked like what you would expect. An open space with bales of hay on one side and empty stalls on the other. Pleasantly surprised, all she could smell was the dry hay, and she figured that no livestock had been housed in here for years. It was two storeys, she established, and next to the stairs that led to the second level, was a large red plastic cooler with a white hinged lid.

"What does your grandfather use this for now?" Rachel asked, walking in further to check out the stalls.

"Surplus mostly," Jamie said, strolling over to the cooler. "Any hay that can't fit in the main barn gets put in here—and up there." He pointed to the stairs, then bent to open the cooler.

She watched as he removed three bottles of water and two full-sized bags of what she recognized as potato chips. She had never been allowed to have any, though she had thought of sneaking some when at the library, and she had seen a few bags stashed in the cupboard when she had put the groceries away for her mother. Had her father been put in jail today, she might have taken a bag, been brave enough to.

"Sorry—I don't have much to offer on food," Jamie said. "I'm the only one who comes here, so I just keep some water and snacks." He grinned. "Are you hungry?"

She was starving actually, now that she had a moment to think about it, and thirsty. "Yes," she said, grinning back. She walked over and took a bag of chips and one of the bottles of water from him.

"Follow me," Jamie said, heading up the stairs.

On the second floor there was a huge opening on the far wall, large enough to fit hay bales stacked ten high and ten wide, and the view from it was breathtaking. It was to her anyway, her *views* had been limited to school, the library, and home. But here, the farmland stretched out bordered by beautiful red maple trees. She understood why he liked to come here. It was peaceful and quiet, and the scenery was spectacular. A breeze blew in through the opening then, causing the old walls of the barn to creak in rhythm with the wind.

She leaned against the framed opening watching as the sun began to lower behind the trees. Then she pulled open the bag of chips and inhaled. The smell of the chips was so intoxicating that she grabbed several up and shoved them into her mouth. She closed her eyes, crunching and savoring the salty crispy goodness. "Chips," she said, exhaling, then turned back to see Jamie spreading a large blanket out over a low stack of hay.

"This is the best," he said, sitting down on the edge of the blanket. "You can see the sun set and then the stars come out from up here." He kicked off his boots and then scooted back on the blanket to lie down. She liked that he wore only a simple white t-shirt and faded blue jeans. She watched as he tucked both his hands behind his head and then exhale in contentment. "You should try it," he added, crossing his legs at the ankles. He wiggled his sock-feet and grinned at her.

"You should try these," she said, referring to the bag of chips in her hand. "These are the best." She gave her eyebrows a couple raises up and down.

"Oh—I know—they're my fave," Jamie said, smacking his lips.

She walked over then to the stack of hay with the blanket and the handsome man now lounged across it and sat down on the edge. Like Jamie had done, she removed her boots and then shifted up the blanket to lie alongside him, chip bag and water bottle in one hand.

As they ate their fancy meal of chips and water, Rachel lay there listening to Jamie tell of the plans he had. "My father wants me to be a cop—go to the academy. I've already been to college, but I want to travel—see different countries, see all the mysteries of the world." She'd never been anywhere, but she'd read about different countries and wonders in many books.

When they were done eating, they both lay in silence, watching the sun slowly set. The colours of yellow, orange, and red were brilliant and blazed like fire. When the sun finally disappeared behind the red maples, the stars began to make their appearance, and a warm breeze blew through the opening into the barn and across their reclined bodies.

Jamie shifted closer to Rachel then, bringing the arm closest to her down along the side of his body, his elbow touching hers. She felt flushed suddenly and sat up. She reached over and took the last water bottle cracked it open and then took a big gulp. Still warm, she wriggled out of Jamie's leather jacket. Balling it up, she placed it at the head of the blanket and rolled back down to put her head on it, the back of her hand grazing his hand then. She took in a long shaky breath.

"Yer safe here, Rachel," Jamie said, as if sensing her anxiety.

She wasn't scared—not in the least, but she was anxious, nervous really. The blood pulsed in her ears as before, but this time it was the good kind of nervous. Not nervous, either she realized, she was excited to be there with him, and she felt free. This is what freedom felt like, and it was coupled with the need to move even closer to him. "I feel… safe," she said in response to him.

Jamie rolled on his side then to face her, resting on his elbow, the side of his head on his hand. "Do you always wear your hair pulled back?" he asked, lifting the end of her long braid off the blanket to examine it closer. "The colour catches in the sun, like gold."

She smiled at that and turned her head to look at him. He smelled good, like fresh laundry and mint. "No," she said, lifting her head and sliding her hair free of his hand to loosen the braid. She mirrored his posture, turning her body then and resting her head on her hand to face him.

"It's beautiful," Jamie said, running his fingers through the loose waves that hung down now. "You're beautiful—did you know that?"

She felt herself flush again. No one had ever called her beautiful before, and she wondered if what she was feeling now—this need to be close to Jamie, was what she'd read about in the romance novels she'd sometimes read at the library. She gazed into his eyes; his face was lit by the moonlight. She had only read about the love and intimacy in books and had never bothered with boys at school—there was no point really, she wasn't even allowed to watch TV let alone have a boyfriend. She kept to herself at school, plus she knew most of the kids thought she was weird, a *loner* the nicer kids had called her. But she knew Jamie was handsome, his features were just like the men she'd read about, and the way he made her feel looking back at her, well… that was what they called *chemistry*, and she was feeling all kinds of science right now.

Jamie's hand moved from her hair then to caress the side of her cheek. His eyes shifted from gazing into hers, down to staring at her mouth. "What are you thinking, Rachel?" he asked then.

"I'm thinking... I should be scared being alone with you... but I'm not." She touched her hand to his. "I'm thinking...." She was thinking she'd been beaten for less, but she was never going back to there again, so what did it matter that she was here alone with him. "... that I never want this night to end."

Jamie licked his lips, then leaned in to brush them against hers. His mouth was soft and warm, and she didn't resist, in fact she leaned in to press her mouth firmly against his. As she did, Jamie's hand slid around to the back of her head to cup it. Rachel's mind raced and her skin heated as if under the rays of the sun. Jamie's touch was so unlike that of her father who commanded, pulled, and shoved in his abuse of her. Jamie's caress was a comfort, one she had never been given, and in this moment Rachel let go, let go of all her anxiety and fears, giving herself over to the feeling of being beautiful, being adored, being a woman, and being *free*.

* * *

Jamie awoke to the sound of a harvest combine grumbling by the barn. They had fallen asleep after, he realized then, rubbing his eyes free of sleep. Sitting up to reach for his jeans and t-shirt, he grasped something else... his leather jacket was gone... and so was Rachel.

Chapter 2

Behind the reporter, a second police car screeched to a halt. "We are here at Oakland Community College here in Auburn Hills," the female reporter said, over the commotion behind her. "Where the unconscious body of the newly hired Professor of Biology, Timothy Armstrong was discovered at the CREST building early this morning. Emergency medical personnel have been called to the scene, but they found no signs of life upon their arrival." The reporter moved to one side as the body in a black coroner's bag was rolled by her. "Based on the injuries sustained, Police are now calling this death a homicide," the reporter continued into the camera. "Sources tell me that all evidence is pointing to the same MO as the notorious serial killer known as the *Small-Town Strangler*. It was 20 years ago, when the killings first began. Back then, after 12 university professors across 12 states were killed, the press had labeled the killings the *Professor Murders*. It has been 6 years since the case file, now known as the Professor's Dozen—still unsolved, went cold. And this latest killing, number 13, makes it a baker's dozen. Where has the killer been all these years—and why have they returned?"

Gwen shook her head and turned away from the reporter to see an unmarked Crown Victoria roll up. This kind of reporting was why she disliked the press. This professor was dead— murdered, and the reporter was treating it like some kind of entertainment piece. "Baker's dozen," she repeated, under her breath.

Gwen was in her last month of training as a paramedic, she had done most of her training here in fact, at this college, right here in the training center. This facility had a combined regional emergency services training program that was set up like a tiny city to provide realistic settings. The trainers took you from the classroom into virtual live lab scenarios based on real-life problems they would be facing as emergency responders. Her instructors and professors here had been amazing, and her paramedic partner, Scott, was an excellent trainer who she had become close friends while on the job. As for the biology class, she had taken the class in her first year here but not with this professor, he'd been new this term. She had heard rumblings that he may have been a little too *handsy* with the female students. Perhaps one of them had had enough, she pondered, watching as Detective Jim Franklin approached their rig.

"Hey, Dad," Scott said, when he had reached the open back doors to the ambulance. It was normal protocol to wait for the police before declaring anyone deceased, and now that the cops were here and dealing with things, they had taken this time to do their own paperwork.

"Good morning! You guys working out of the Oakland location?" Detective Franklin asked.

"Ya, we got the call to come here," Scott said. "Some poor student found the professor and called 911, and they dispatched us to the scene, but the guy was gone—no signs of life, when we got here.

"Hey, Gwen, how's the training going? My son getting you ready to take on the world?" He had his hands on his hips in a way that reminded her of a superhero stance.

"Hi, Detective Franklin—yes, I'm learning from the Jedi Master," she said, with a chuckle.

"What can you tell me about the victim's injuries?" Detective Franklin asked, directing the question at her. He'd most likely already heard the scoop or he would not be here, but he liked to be part of the training process any chance he got. He planned to teach at this facility when he retired from the force, Scott had told her, and she felt he would make an excellent addition to the staff here.

"We found ligature marks around his neck, but not from a rope—something wider," she said, pausing. She had heard about the serial killer when she'd been in high school, but when no other murders that matched were found, the story had disappeared from the news and she'd forgotten about it until Scott had mentioned it to her awhile back, when she'd first met Detective Franklin. "And he'd been tasered," she added, this had been part of the original MO of this killer, she had remembered. She also recalled what Scott had told her about his father, well— stepfather, and how he had met and married Scott's mother, Gayle, 15 years ago. He had officially adopted Scott after marrying his mom, and Scott had taken his last name. Scott was 25 now, but when he was fresh out of training, he remembered then how distraught his stepfather had been when this case had gone cold. Scott had told her that his stepfather had been working this case in one capacity or another almost since the beginning. When he was Scott's age, he had moved up the ranks fast, and when the murders began traveling across the country, he'd followed the case as a homicide detective. In 2003 he had been recognized for his collective experience as a specialist on the case and had been teamed to work in conjunction with the FBI. He had worked other cases over the years, but he had never given up hope that he'd find this elusive small-town strangler.

"Same MO," Detective Franklin said, to his son.

"Same MO," Scott said back, jumping down from the rig, confirming what they had all concluded.

"You guys have time for some breakfast or coffee?" Detective Franklin asked, glancing back and forth at the two of them.

Scott shut the back doors to the ambulance. "Overnight shift is done," Scott said. "I just need to swap vehicles and then I can meet you at the diner. Gwen—you in?"

Gwen hopped down from the back of the ambulance and shut the doors. "You bet—I'm starving," she said, then opened the passenger side door of the rig to get in. She gave the detective the thumbs up, then climbed in and shut the door. "Let's go!" she said, through the open window on her side, reaching out and giving the outside of the door a double giddy-up smack with her hand.

"Okay see you there," the detective responded.

In the hospital ambulance bay, they locked up their rig, turned in their respective paperwork, and then climbed into Scott's blue and grey 1994 Ford Bronco. He and Detective Franklin had restored it, still worked on it when they had a day off together, and it was his pride and joy. She couldn't blame him, it was a great truck, and she had no car to speak of and was always thankful for a lift.

On the ride over to the diner, Gwen thought about the last time she had crossed paths with Detective Franklin during her training. It had been a month ago on an exceptionally warm night—her third shift in a row—and she still had yet to become accustomed to the level of exhaustion, when she and Scott had been super busy with all kinds of calls. It was in the University District at just after 2 a.m., outside an old brick colonial home adjacent to one which had obviously been managed through the heritage society because that one was immaculate, this one they were heading into had not, it had been changed into a halfway house for troubled homeless youths.

The first thing she'd noted when they'd entered, was that it was as hot inside as it was out, and they had to climb two flights of stairs to get to the third floor of the place. The stair railings were solid dark wood like the trim in the house but had clearly been painted over several times, and the floors and stairs creaked with every step. The place had smelled like pot and incense, and everywhere it was dimly lit.

On the landing, she'd seen that the bedroom they were heading into was one of three, along with a small bathroom on that level, and there were at least three teenage girls up there they could see, each sobbing quietly and keeping their distance. There must have been another girl in one of the rooms out of view because they could hear her heartbroken wailing.

When she and Scott had entered the bedroom through the doorway that was offset in the corner of the room, she'd seen a small side table covered with a silk scarf with a small lamp and several artists' pencils were atop it. There'd been a large queen-sized bed with colourful blankets and pillows on it but the colours had been dimmed from the pale lighting. There had been a lot of stuff on the walls, art, more scarves, posters. The foot of the bed had a short white bookshelf full of books by *Stephen King*, paperback, hard cover, and even those with his pen-name *Richard Bachman*. Around the other side of the bed, along the same wall as the table and the headboard, there had been a tiny door to a closet.

The door had been propped open and inside hanging amidst the clothes, the colourful hippy-style flowing skirts and loose-fitting blouses, facing towards the right of the closet, was a small-statured teenage girl. Gwen had only been able to see her from her right side, but her head was tilted forward as though nodding *yes*. She'd had short pixie hair, noticeably shorter in the back almost shaved, with longer bits at the sides that had perfectly circled the outline of her face along her jaw. To this day, Gwen still couldn't recall what the girl had hung herself with or what she was wearing, but the top of her head had been right up against the bar where she had secured the noose, and her toes… they had been only a fraction of an inch from the ground. The girl could have easily stretched a bit and stopped this if she had wanted.

Scott had been attending to this call, so he had checked the girl's right arm, starting at the fingers, then wrist, and then the elbow, checking for rigor mortis, and he had found it at the elbow. *"She's cool to the touch,"* he had told her, realizing that the girl was obviously dead and there was nothing they could do. This had then become a crime scene, and they had needed to notify police. Scott had backed away from the closet, then had turned her around so they could both leave the room. *"You'll see enough of this in your career—you don't need to start it off with this,"* he had said to her.

When they'd been leaving the room, she'd noticed the books again. She had read those same books because she was also a *Stephen King* fan, and she also folded the corners of the pages of her books instead of using a book marker like the girl had. Gwen had internalized and empathized with this dead girl's personality very quickly and paired with the emotions of the other girls in the house, tears had begun to stream down her face. She'd kept her head low and excused herself to go outside. At the truck, she had gathered herself by the time the police had arrived, and Detective Franklin had shown up. He had gone to speak to Scott first, but then he had come over to see her, and had asked if she was okay. Scott had obviously seen her tears and had told him. *"Scott has this covered—no need for you to stay up there with all that sadness,"* he'd said. Then he had gone on to tell her the girl's tragic story, about an 18-year-old with a debilitating illness and anxiety over revealing her sexuality to an estranged family at an upcoming gathering. The young girl they had heard wailing from the other bedroom had been her girlfriend, she hadn't heard from her partner in several days. Then one of the housemates, who had feared the worst, had then come in and found her.

That had been Gwen's roughest call to date, but Detective Franklin had been exceptionally kind with her that time. She hadn't cried again, but she'd been pretty shaken up and he'd taken the time to explain, how the job can get to you at times, and that she shouldn't be afraid to reach out and talk to someone if needed. He had reminded her that Scott had seen some pretty horrific stuff his first year, and that he had made a point of talking to the counselor they had on staff. Detective Franklin had known just what to do, and what to say, to make her feel better. She had never had a father, but she was more than grateful for the comfort he'd given her then, and she had never forgotten it.

In the back of a small Ann Arbor bakery, news coverage barked out details through a small TV set on a side table. "This latest murder makes the total thirteen now," the male reporter stated.

"Noooo, god—no, he's back," Laura Jamison said, with a gasp.

Chapter 3

Laura had been in Lewisburg for almost a year now, but she had moved four times in the three years prior, since the killings had started, though she had yet to receive another postcard.

She had received a postcard shortly after every move, each one sent from the town she had lived prior, even though she had never left a forwarding address with anyone. They were never signed, always had a photo on the front of some popular landmark from the last city she had lived in, and all handwritten on the back with the same message,

> *Welcome to your new home, Laura.*
> *I killed that professor for you. Please don't contact the police, you will NOT live to regret it. Remember, I'm watching you.*
> *Enjoy your stay!*

Each time she moved she ran through the same routine of setting up her personal security. She had learned a lot about how to secure her tiny apartments, from checking the lighting in all areas to simple fixes for doors and windows that she could obtain from any hardware store.

Apartment buildings and complexes sometimes had dark nooks and crannies she'd noticed, making it perfect for anyone who wanted to sneak around. It's important to have good lighting in common areas like hallways, garbage areas, stairwells, laundry rooms and parking areas, not that she had a car, but having to walk through them, it made sense to note the lighting. She preferred smaller apartment complexes, with fewer than eight units, usually renting on the first floor. A first-floor unit may make it easier for an intruder to get in, but it also made it easier for her to get out, and was especially good for moving in and out, she had found. If she had to take a higher floor, she always considered the emergency exits, making sure she could get out in case of any danger.

Securing any doors or windows had become a cinch now that she had done it multiple times. First was the security hinge with tamper-proof pins and a locking tab for doors. If she was in a position where she couldn't do that, she had several more options that she more than often combined, like door chains that allowed the doors to be opened slightly to see outside while still remaining locked, these were good when you didn't have a peep hole. Her favorite was the pick-proof deadbolt, because even an amateur intruder could pick a lock, she'd read, and using the sliding lock over the deadbolt's handle, keeps it from turning. Lastly were the windows. For those she used pin locks which she had found were an easy solution. She'd bought a cheap drill to install them, and she'd learned from the guy at the hardware store that if you wanted to lock a window in a partially opened position, you need only drill a second hole. Which was handy if you wanted some fresh air without risking the security. On more than one occasion she had had the sense that someone was following her, and she was a single mother now, the last thing she needed, was someone coming in through an unlocked or wide-open window.

Several years back, when she had gotten her first bakery job, the owner had given her a travel trunk to keep her belongings in. It was one of those rectangular ones with engineered wood construction, a heavy gauge vinyl covering and a paper-lined interior to protect contents, making it a reliable solution for all her storage or travel needs as it were. It was the wheeled footlocker type, 30 inches wide, 15 across and 12 deep, with black high impact bindings, nickel plated hardware and two durable recessed wheels. It had a side carry handle and a front one to make moving the trunk simple. It also had an easy open push button key lock. The keys had been lost prior to her owning the trunk, but it could also be locked with a padlock for added security. And she had dragged that thing with her each time she had had to leave and move to a new town.

She hadn't owned much when she'd started out, but she had accumulated some basic kitchen stuff; two pots, one large, one small, a single egg fry pan, a small toaster, some baking tools, a roll-up knife set and even a food processor—second hand of course, along with essentials for the baby, paired with the home items that came with a basic furnished rental, and she believed she had everything she needed. She also had a notebook which she kept her recipes in, ones she had learned and the ones she'd invented herself. And like this place, the small towns she preferred to live in, had everything she felt she needed too, usually within walking distance, plus a few extras beyond what she required.

There was the grocery store, it was always nice having easy access to food and arguably one of the most important businesses in town. Like the grocery store, pharmacies played a vital role for her as well. In addition to prescriptions, the needs of the community essentially determined what else they had in stock, like over the counter medication, baby formula, toiletries, vitamins, and whatever, it varied from town to town, she had found. She guessed a hair salon was needed in each town too, almost everyone needed a haircut at one point or another, but she had trimmed her own hair for years and normally wore it pulled back and in a bun since she worked in food services. The hardware store and a local handyman were two other staples in small towns. Every town needs a local handyman, and she had learned plenty from the guys at the hardware stores.

Now a laundromat, if you were not fortunate enough to have a washer and dryer in your building, this was essential, especially with a baby. She didn't own many clothes, so other than towels and bedding, and the baby stuff, that was all she had that required constant washing.

There always seemed to be an auto repair shop/gas station combo in every town she moved to. There is no denying that every small town needs a gas station, and a mechanic, but it wasn't on her list of necessities — no car, no need, she didn't even have a driver's license. Bus services had been her means of transportation, and like gas stations, every town had a bus station, even if it was just a sign next to the gas station that also sold the tickets.

Along with the gas station, there was always at least one bar. She knew that bars often had things like pool tables and dartboards, but even if she were interested in these things, bringing a baby into a bar was surely frowned upon. It was the gathering place to talk about the day's news or catch up with an old friend apparently, but she didn't have any friends and she definitely didn't have any news to share, plus she had no interest in drinking.

Restaurants, every town needed them, but not every town needed every type of restaurant. A good pizza shop, a place that served a good breakfast, and one of those all-American restaurants that serves good burgers and fries, was probably enough, in her view, and the eat-in bakery café she worked at, of course. Excess was not something she respected, probably because she lived a minimalist life, only spending what she needed and buying only the essentials, everything else she felt was a luxury. Not to say she didn't want a better life for her and her child but spending her well-earned money on frivolous things wasn't going to get her or take her anywhere. Slow and steady wins the race, she had told herself.

It wasn't a necessity, but she preferred the towns that had a college or university in them. She would have loved to go to college but being a single mother had taken precedence. Bucknell University was founded in 1846 and featured a multitude of programs, and even had a Female Institute, though despite being opened in 1852, it hadn't been until 1883 that college courses were opened to women, and she couldn't quite understand that. Her boss had suggested that she take a night course there. She'd not had very good success with that in the past, though she loved visiting the college to walk the grounds.

She was looking forward to the cherry blossoms that bloomed in April on the Academic Quad near the Bertrand Library where she often liked to walk. It was a 450-acre campus with numerous Georgian style brick buildings that ran adjacent to the West Branch Susquehanna River. The campus was divided into Lower and Upper Campuses and it offered amazing views northwest across the Buffalo Valley toward Nittany Mountain and southeast across the Susquehanna River toward Montour Ridge. They had a non-denominational Chapel on campus for worship, weddings, and celebrations, which she thought was very progressive, not that she needed any of those things. And there's the Christy Mathewson-Memorial Stadium, the home to the Bucknell University Bison football team and the Lewisburg

High School Green Dragons football team. Again, not something she needed, but it was a morale booster for the town.

Another thing she was looking forward to in April, was that her daughter would be turning *four*, her terrible twos had continued into the threes, and she was hopeful they would finally be past this difficult stage. She had been a good baby, actually, but there was something about turning two that had sparked some defiance in her daughter, her favorite word being *No*, which had ignited a few choice words of her own—that Laura had luckily managed to keep under her breath, a challenge thus far. Laura knew that moving so much had not been easy on either of them, but she did her best to provide some joy for her daughter. Stability on the other hand, well, that was another challenge she was working through.

Thankfully, when she had moved here last year, she had once again managed to secure a job, and she had found a first-floor apartment in a three-story brownstone just off the university's campus. The other tenants in the building were students at Bucknell, one of them was gone most of the time, and the other was doing a minor in Women's Gender Studies and though Laura had found her very interesting to talk to, she had also found someone willing and trustworthy to watch her daughter when she had to work the breakfast and lunch shift. She had been able to bring her daughter with her on overnight shifts since there were no customers during those times.

The coffee shop/bakery—where she currently worked, seemed typical now of every small town. If you were a coffee lover, this was the place to go. Apparently 64% of Americans over the age of 18 drink coffee regularly. She wasn't one to drink much coffee, but she would guarantee that each customer would be greeted with a smile and a great cup of coffee, and hopefully one of her pastries. She had made a point to always be vigilant, watching her surroundings, the people, the ones she didn't recognize, and even the ones she knew.

The customer coming in now, unfortunately, she did recognize. It was *Professor Complainer*. Laura had been told that he taught at the university, something in the Foods Systems program, but despite coming in and eating there every day, he always felt the need to share a negative remark about the food each time. The staff had joked about poisoning his food, or at least adding a little something to make him sick, keep him out of commission and out of the place for a few days or so. Laura rarely worked at the order side of the counter, but she was covering for the young girl who normally did, while she took a break. Lucky her, Laura thought, as their favorite customer approached the order area. "Good morning," Laura said, with a smile. "What can we make for you today, sir?" She waited while he reviewed the specials and the regular menu board. He had only been reading the same things every day, but he clearly wanted to make her and the customers behind him wait. *Arrogant prick,* she had wanted to say, but she held her smile.

"Let me seeee," he said, drawing out the last word.

Laura couldn't help herself, she let out a loud sigh due to the frustrated breath she'd been holding.

"Oh—I'm sorry, am I keeping you from something? Baking crap food and brewing crap coffee, perhaps?"

Laura bit the corner of her lip. "No-no, Sir. What can I get for you?"

And then like normal, he ordered his usual. "Large coffee—black, and a raspberry croissant." Laura grimaced. "Is there something wrong?" he asked, his voice raising.

"No—it's just that we sold the last raspberry croissant. Could I offer you something else?" Laura rocked from foot to foot.

"Something else? The raspberry croissant is the only thing barely edible in this place," he said, his voice raising even higher now. "Just the coffee—see if you can get that right for a change." He tossed a dollar on the counter; a large coffee was 0.95 cents.

"Thank you," Laura said, through the gritted teeth of her smile. At least she didn't have to hand it to him, the food pick-up area was at the other end of the counter, and the person preparing the order would have to deal with him, which would have typically been her if she hadn't been covering the cash. Timing was everything, she thought to herself.

* * *

The next morning, when Laura arrived outside of work, there was a small crowd gathering at the corner near the bakery. She could see the local news reporters standing with their mics out and cameramen at the ready. They seemed to be waiting on the police chief and another taller dark-haired man not in uniform, who she could only see the back of, to make an announcement of some kind.

Laura hurried into the shop and caught the arm of the cashier. "What's going on?" she asked the girl.

"You didn't see the news this morning?" The girl said, leaning to look out the window.

"No—what, what happened?" Laura turned to see where the girl was looking.

"Right—no TV, sorry," the girl said, clearly remembering that Laura didn't have a TV at home.

There was one in the back of the bakery that she and the other baker flipped on once in a while, but she didn't usually watch the local news. Laura readily used local newspapers to find apartments, and jobs, as well as the online newspapers at the local library to follow any news on the serial killings. But no news was good news, wasn't it?

"That professor—the one we all love so much, he's dead," she tossed out. "The police are making an announcement about it to the press."

"Why?" Laura asked, then shivered, a little tingle prickling the back of her neck.

"Why is he dead?" the girl asked, "or why are they making a statement to the press?"

"The press," Laura said, she didn't care why the guy was dead, but the tingle at the back of her neck now traveling down her spine, was an indicator that the next words out of this girl's mouth would be something she may not want to know—but needed to know.

"They brought in a homicide specialist. Seems the evidence indicates it was murder and the same MO as that serial killer, *the small-town strangler*," she said, leaning again to look out the shop window as the crowd continued to gather.

Just then the owner of the shop came out from the back bakery. "The cops are gonna want to speak to each of us," she said, to Laura and the other staff now gathering near the window.

"Why us," Laura questioned, wrapping her arms around herself though she wasn't cold.

"One of the customers told the cops he'd been in here causing a ruckus." She rolled her eyes. "That asshole professor caused us grief every morning—yesterday was no exception. But if the cops think it can help—we can each spare a few minutes to help them and the FBI solve a murder, can't we? Kind of exciting—if you ask me," she added, peeking out the window.

* * *

In the days that followed, each of the staff was taken to the back office of the bakery to be interviewed by the local police. Laura had cooperated by telling them about the last time she had seen the professor, the morning prior to his death and about the exchange they had had. The others had mentioned it to the cop interviewing them, so she was merely confirming what the others had already said. None of them could be guilty of the murder, but that fact hadn't put her at ease.

All week she'd had the sense that someone was following her, and it only escalated her unease. Then twice she had found the window in the front of her apartment left open without the pin lock in it, and she had even found the front door left unlocked once. Laura had given the student watching her daughter a key to the apartment, because she liked to go from her apartment to Laura's when babysitting, that it helped entertain her daughter, she'd told Laura, but when she questioned her about the window and door, she'd explained that she never opens the windows and always locks the door when she leaves. Laura had wanted to believe the girl, but these violations of her security—if her babysitter hadn't done them, she wanted to know then, who had?

The panic this had caused Laura only worsened when she had found the new postcard that had been slid under her apartment door. This one hadn't been a 'welcome' message like the others, but it did have a warning similar to the ones she had received,

> *Enjoying your stay?*
> *You know I killed that professor for you, but you spoke to the police despite my previous warnings. Don't let that happen again.*
> *Remember, I'm watching you, AND your daughter.*

She'd had no choice but to talk to the police, she hadn't instigated the contact. The killer must have known this, or they would not have given her this second chance to keep her mouth shut. Laura took this warning even more seriously than the first ones, because unlike the others that had images of the places she lived prior, this one had a photo of Bucknell University on it and it had been purchased at the university's tuck shop, she'd seen this exact one on her last visit. But the warning had hit home more than this postcard being from the town she currently lived in, it had been more obvious than that, and now any ideas she had entertained about speaking further to the cops, telling them what she knew—all that she'd been going through, had been thoroughly eradicated from her thought process, because there was only one thing that mattered about this postcard, and it was the fact that the killer's message, had mentioned her *daughter*.

Chapter 4

July 1st, 2019 - Royal Oak Diner, Royal Oak, MI

"How are you feeling about that call this morning?" Detective Franklin asked, as Gwen and Scott slid into the booth seat across from him.

"Weird," Scott said, straightening the paper placemat.

What was weird to Gwen, was being here. She and Scott had been to this diner before, they only lived up the street, but this was the first time she had been anywhere with the detective, other than on the job. "Ya, it's strange to get called to such familiar ground, let alone establish that someone's been murdered," Gwen said, shooting a glance at Scott. "I mean, I don't technically go there anymore—to the college. I don't have any more classes—just this last month of on the job training, but it was my home away from home for the past three years."

"Call locations are not usually so… *personal*," Scott added.

"Well, this one feels personal to me too," Detective Franklin said, "but not in the same way." He motioned for the waitress, asking for her to fill his coffee cup.

"You two want anything?" the waitress asked, as she filled the detective's cup.

"Coffee," Scott said.

"Me too, please," Gwen said, sliding her coffee cup over. "And can I get a fried egg sandwich—on brown?"

"Sure thing," the waitress said, pouring their coffees next.

When the waitress left, Detective Franklin said, "I don't know how much Scott has told you, Gwen." He sipped his coffee. "But I've been working this case almost since its inception. Time in, makes it personal for me—nearly 20 years of my life I've been chasing this bastard—sorry, this guy," he said, correcting his words as if to be more polite.

"Bastard is more accurate," she said, as she added cream to her coffee, cooling it down. She didn't know how the detective could drink it, being so hot. *Badass*, she thought. Scott on the other hand had added three sugars and most of the creamers to his.

Detective Franklin nodded at her comment, then said, "This latest murder—I couldn't believe it when I saw the evidence report." He sipped the scalding coffee again. "He's here—killing in my county," he added, leaning in as if to avoid being overheard. "Six years I've been waiting—six years. You hope for a new lead—any lead, but never for someone to be killed." He ran a hand through his shot cropped hair.

This was seriously personal for him; Gwen had only truly realized now. "Yer gonna find him, Detective—I just know it," she said, just as the waitress arrived with her food. Gwen had had an idea, through Scott, about the length of time his father had been on this case, and this had to be the turning point for him.

Scott eyeballed her food. "Sorry—Miss," he said, to the woman twice his age. "Could I get the same?" He gave her a boyish grin.

She grinned back and gave him a little wink. "Anything for you, sweetheart," she said, then hustled off to fill the order.

Gwen smacked him on the arm. "What? She loves me—what can I say," Scott said, rubbing his upper arm.

"You're not eating anything, Detective?" Gwen asked, as she dispensed a blob of ketchup on her plate.

"Naw-naw—I like to eat breakfast with my wife, when I can. She'll be waking up soon," he said, checking his watch. "She'd love to see you for dinner—sometime soon, Scott."

Gwen smacked him on the arm again.

"Ouch, you're one to talk—when was the last time you saw your mom?" Scott countered, picking up his knife and fork as if to use them for weapons.

"Ya-ya, I know," Gwen said, knowing she was due for a visit with her own mother. Redirecting the topic, she asked, "Sir, where did this all start—I mean, how did you get involved?" She stared at the detective over the rim of her coffee cup as she took a long sip, then said, "Did you always want to be a cop?"

"Did I always want to be a cop? No—but I knew pretty early on that I wanted to solve mysteries," he said. "I didn't want to be a regular cop—not that it's a bad thing, it just wasn't what I wanted to do."

"Did you grow up in Detroit?" Gwen asked, curious now what drove this man to devote so much of his life to this case.

"Nope, I'm from a small town, but I moved to the big city of Detroit because I didn't want to be a small-town cop. Something happened in my hometown—that made me want to solve crimes, not just protect citizens from them."

"Were you living in the same town as the first murder—the first of the serial murders?" Gwen asked, her next question already waiting.

Scott's food arrived, and Detective Franklin seem to be waiting until the waitress was gone before answering, then he leaned in and said, "The first murder was in Hanover, New Hampshire in the fall of 1998, and less than an hour from where I grew up. I had already completed my degree in Criminal Justice and had only just completed my training at the police academy when I'd initially heard about it. It wasn't considered a serial case back then yet." He leaned back. "Have you ever thought of becoming a police detective—you seem like this might be just up your alley," he added, with a grin.

"Ha—not a chance, but I love a good mystery," Gwen said, then took another bite of her food, totally engrossed and ready for more.

"You and Dad will get along great then," Scott said, cutting in between bites of his own breakfast.

Detective Franklin went on, relaying the details of the initial murder. A professor of course, this one was from the Art History Department at Dartmouth College, an Ivy League college with quite the reputation and Hanover had been ranked the sixth best place to live in the country. "They'd had no leads, but students had come forward saying they heard that the professor could get a bit too touchy-feely with the female students," he said.

"Much like this professor," Gwen added.

"Guess you heard that part too then," Detective Franklin said.

"Ya—that kind of thing gets around these days," Scott said, pushing his plate to the side.

"Do you think a student could be responsible for this?" Gwen asked.

"Not if this is part of the serial case—which it seems to be," the detective responded. "They'd be too young to have committed the other murders."

"A parent maybe—a father? Word does get around. Maybe this guy has a daughter who was harassed by the professor, maybe his mother—or a sister of his had been harassed by that original professor—and that started him on his spree," Gwen suggested.

"So, what—this guy goes from town to town, waiting to see if any professors harass female students and then he kills them?" Scott said, debunking Gwen's theory.

"Got any better ideas?" she asked, play stabbing his hand with her fork.

"Are you sure you guys aren't related—you argue like siblings," Detective Franklin, said with a hearty laugh.

"She wishes," Scott said, squishing her into the corner of the booth. He had her by at least a hundred pounds. He was built like a tank, played rugby in high school, and still went faithfully to the gym.

She had played volleyball, not quite a contact sport, and she was tall, like her mother, not as tall as he was but still. She shoved him back, tried to at least. "We don't look anything alike," Gwen said. They didn't, he had a square face, hers was oval, his eyes were pale blue, hers were brown, her hair was strawberry blond and his was brown, but she thought of him as someone she would have liked to have known growing up, since she hadn't had many friends, nor any siblings.

"Where does your mom live?" the detective asked.

"She's just out of town in Ann Arbor, but she grew up in Cambridge, Massachusetts. My grandmother still lives there.

"That's where I'm originally from." He leaned in again. "What's your mother's name?"

"Oh, you might know her, Laura Jamison," Gwen said.

"Hmmm doesn't ring a bell. How old is she?" the detective asked, rubbing his jaw.

"She turned 40 this past April." Gwen at the last bit of her meal, then pushed her plate to the side, to invade Scott's side of the table.

Detective Franklin shook his head. "Ya—no, we wouldn't have been in school together back then. And I don't recognize the name." He shrugged.

Gwen shrugged. She hadn't known much about her mother's past, and her mom didn't talk about it. She didn't talk much about anything from her life, not even Gwen's father. All she knew was that he had died in a car crash shortly after he and her mother had gotten married, he wouldn't have even known Gwen existed at the time of his death.

Drawing Gwen's attention back, Detective Franklin said, "It wasn't until the next two murders, one at Bowdoin College in Brunswick, Maine, and the other at Middlebury College in Middlebury Vermont, that the feds realized that they had a serial killer on their hands."

Chapter 5

September 1ˢᵗ, 2008 - Charlottesville, Virginia

When they had first moved to Charlottesville, Laura had swiftly secured a new job at a family run chain-style bakery, and she had found a new place for them to live in a four-plex. Their new place was on the first floor with a shared front door for all the units, but out back they each had their own space, the bottom floors being porches and the upper units being balconies. Laura had been hesitant at first with the two entrances, communal front and personal back, but having the back porch and yard, tiny as it was, it had provided them a nice space to sit outside they had not had before.

Laura had hated that Gwen had to finish out her school year in a new place but there had not been much Laura could do about it. Knowing that Gwen made friends easily, she had breathed a sigh of relief when she had made friends with the little boy and girl next door on the same floor as them. The back porches had only a long skinny planter to divide them and the yard space was more like one big fenced-in space for the kids to play. The two kids had even offered to walk with Gwen to school each day. It was just up the street, but Laura had found some comfort in the three walking together. And their mother, a bit down and out and on social assistance, was a respectful woman, and had given Laura plenty of privacy when they had moved in.

As the school year ended, the little girl next door was having a birthday party, and Gwen had been invited. The party had been mostly girls, the little brother the only boy, eight kids in total, and it was then that Laura realized, Gwen preferred the company of the little boy over the girls, as she had played with him the whole time. Gwen was a bit of a tomboy, which made boys more appealing to play with, Laura had guessed. Either way, Laura was happy if Gwen was happy. Until she wasn't, Gwen that is.

The fall of that same year, in the second week of the new school year, Laura received a call to come to the school. When she'd arrived, the vice principle explained that Gwen and the neighbor boy and another little boy had been playing some game that Gwen had been winning at, the other boy upset at not winning, had said something to upset Gwen. Both her neighbor and the mother of the other boy had been called in too. Apparently, the boy had said something about how Gwen was a loser because she didn't have a father. That's when Gwen had yelled at the kid, saying, *"We don't need a father, do we?"* Referring to herself and the neighbor boy. Then she had punched the kid hard, which is what had actually gotten her in trouble and why the parents had been called down to the school.

When Gwen was brought into the office, she had entered wiping her eyes using both hands, and Laura could tell her daughter had been crying.

"Well they don't—have fathers," the other boy's mother said, before Laura had a chance to even speak to her daughter.

Laura and the neighbor glared back at the woman, then Laura said, "Gwen, you are not to play with that little boy again." Then she turned her daughter to go back out the door.

"My son won't be playing with your son either," her neighbor said, as she followed the Laura and Gwen out.

On the walk home, the neighbor expressed that both Laura and her daughter were kind and personable, but still private, and that would not do well with making friends around here. She also said she knew that people liked to pry, but she wasn't one of them. Laura had liked the neighbor, liked that she rarely made any negative comments despite her circumstances, and she had liked her even more after that.

Later that night, after the kids had been put to bed, Laura and the neighbor sat out on their respective back porches, chatting. The neighbor shared with Laura about her kids' father, about how she'd had to escape an abusive marriage, literally change states, with the assistance of a government funded program she'd found, and that she and her kids were doing great now and were all better off without him.

Laura found a connection and a sense of security with what her neighbor had shared, and Laura chose to share her story as well. She explained that Gwen's father had died before Gwen had been born, had left her with nothing, how they'd been young when they had gotten married, how she'd moved around a lot, and how it had been hard finding work at times. But she also told her how she loved working in the baking industry, and that her daughter was happy here. "Gwen is resilient—more than me," she said to her new friend.

"You should try for more courses," the neighbor suggested to her.

Laura had been intrigued by the idea, though another year went by before she was brave enough to take the plunge.

The University of Virginia was another one of those small-town schools Laura loved so much, and had been founded by Thomas Jefferson in 1819, not that that was important to Laura, she had just found it interesting. The school had a multitude of programs, but Laura was only interested in the state funded evening cooking classes they offered, the ones her neighbor had told her about. She liked the idea of expanding her cooking knowledge outside of her baking skills, and she enrolled that September.

By Christmas she had completed her first intensive course. It had been harder than she'd expected but she'd learned a lot, and as a small bonus, the class worked together on the last day, to prepare a variety of holiday specialties for their own little holiday party.

Laura had been enjoying the food and the comradery with the other women from the class, when she'd heard a voice from behind her say, "Men are better cooks—we all know that. But women, I'd allow them to still work in the field." When Laura turned around, she saw a fat fifty-something man, with a greasy face, wearing a bad suit, going from serving dish to serving dish, sticking his finger in each and then lifting the finger to taste each one. Luckily, they had all had their servings, but it had still been disgusting to watch. He hadn't used a napkin to wipe off his hands, instead he wiped the saliva covered finger he'd used across the front of his suit jacket, then he'd dipped it into the next pot, and so on.

One of the other women from the class glanced over at Laura, and said, "Another one of those professors who doesn't practice what they preach."

"What?" Laura asked.

"You know, those who can't—teach. He teaches The Politics of Food class here." She rolled her eyes.

The man seemed to think he owned the place and had glowered at Laura while he licked his fingers from the last dish. It took everything she had not to throw up right there. She chose then to make her excuse to leave and say her goodbyes to the teacher and the other students. She had been having fun, but she needed to go, needed the comfort of her home and to see Gwen snug in her bed. When she got home, she'd carried Gwen into her bed to sleep with her. She had felt uneasy about something, something that she couldn't quite put her finger on.

In the morning, as she headed out the door with Gwen, she ran into her favorite neighbor. "How was the last night?" the neighbor asked.

"*Good*," she said, handing Gwen off to walk with the other two kids.

When the kids were out of earshot, the neighbor said, "Did you hear about the professor? He taught in the same building where you took your course." The neighbor crossed her arms over her chest.

"Which professor," Laura asked, worried something might have happened to her teacher. She scanned the street, glancing right then left.

"Dead—they thought it was a heart attack, but the cops say it's murder," she told her, leading against one of the posts that held up the tiny front porch roof.

Laura's worry turned suddenly to dread. "Not the guy who teaches Politics of Food?"

"Ya—that's the one—why, did you know him?" she asked.

"No-no, I didn't," Laura sputtered out, feeling sick suddenly.

"Good, because I hear he was a real pig," she said, then snorted, "looked like one too in the photo they showed on the news."

"I gotta go," Laura said, moving her satchel off her shoulder, instead to cross over her chest, then she rushed down the front steps and off to work.

Later, when she returned home from work, she found a postcard in her mailbox, had almost been expecting it, but what she hadn't expected, was what had been written in the message.

It had said,

Congratulations on completing your course!

As a reward, I killed that professor for you. And I'm going to let you stay here for a while.

Just don't get too comfortable, and remember, no police, or you and your daughter will NOT live to regret it.

I see you, Laura. I'm watching you both.

Enjoy your reward!

Murder was not a reward. But being able to stay, was, because the owners at her job had been impressed with the assistance Laura had given them with developing a new line of savory goods for the bakery.

The line went on to be successful for both the local sales and distributed, and as a result, Laura had been asked to oversee it and any new development. And over the next two years, along with running the development for the bakery, Laura had been able to learn the production and distribution side of things with the company. As an added bonus, thankfully, Laura had heard no news regarding any new murders, nor had she heard anything from her stalker. Though that hadn't been the case with her moves prior.

In Lewisburg back in 2002, despite hearing the news about the murder, she had stayed for an additional year that time. She hadn't been in a position to move right away, and with the obvious changes in the messages from her sick stalker, the focus now on her daughter, she had felt it best not to throw suspicion her way and keep the cops at bay. If she had taken off right after the murder like she'd done previously, it would have looked sketchy why, and considering she had been the one who had talked to the victim that day, it may have looked as though she had a motive or had been somehow involved. And in a way, she had been.

She had information that could be vital to the cops, but what could she have told them, that some guy had been following her across the country, killing professors as devotional tokens of some sort? All that would have done was given her unwanted attention, put her daughter in the spotlight, and possibly enrage this stalker to take things to another level, potentially hurting her and her daughter, or worse. She hated knowing someone was out there killing people, but she couldn't risk it. Maybe it had been selfish, but she had only one goal, and that was to keep her daughter safe. The following January, she had been better prepared to move again. In Baltimore, Maryland, she had found a place to live and had secured another job at a bakery.

The owners had been impressed with her skills and work ethic, but what they had really needed was someone to help manage the place as well. Into her first month at the bakery, the owners had suggested Laura take some business courses, that they would even pay for them. She hadn't wanted to pass up the opportunity, so she had enrolled in one of the evening classes that had been starting that month.

When March rolled in, she had been in her glory, working the morning shift while her daughter attended school, her afternoons were spent with Gwen, and evenings spent attending class or working on her homework. The place she had rented was the upper level of a duplex, though she would have preferred the lower, the landlord and owner of the place occupied the first floor. The older woman clearly hadn't needed the rent money, and Laura had been convinced that renting to someone had been more about wanting the company, because she had invited them for supper that first night when they'd moved in, and later, when Laura had told her about the night classes, she'd generously offered to watch Gwen for her anytime. Between her job, the paid-for night classes at the local university, and the built-in babysitter, all things considered, Laura had felt her new setup was a win, win, *win*.

Notre Dame of Maryland University offered Maryland's only women's college, as well as certificate, undergraduate, graduate, and PhD programs for both women and men. The course handout had boasted that for 125 years, *Their approach to education has prepared thousands of high performers and instigators of social change, and that they were consistently responsive to the needs of a student body hungry to learn, and a world hungry for knowledgeable compassionate leaders.* That, *They embodied pioneering educational tradition and a social justice mission that spurred the College of Notre Dame to welcome the first class of women pursuing a four-year baccalaureate degree in 1895*, and *Their transformative educational model will help prepare you for leadership and success.* She had been nervous about taking classes, but after reading the pamphlet, she had thought, how could she go wrong?

Laura had loved the class and the instructor, but on the regular night she attended the college, she had noticed students coming and going from an office with the placard labeled Professor of International Business. It wasn't the students coming and going that had bothered her, it was the fact that it had been a different *female* student each time, that they had always appeared to be flustered, fixing their clothing, adjusting their skirts or hair or whatever.

In April, the same week as Gwen's 5th birthday, on the last day of Laura's course, she'd chosen to turn left this time to take the exit nearest the professor's office, rather than turn right for her regular route out of the building. She understood it was none of her business, but it was obvious to her what had been going on in that office all those other nights. And as she approached, like clockwork, the door to the office had opened and another girl had exited. But this time along with the rearranging of clothes, this girl had been crying. The girl took off quickly when she'd seen Laura approaching, but it had given Laura just enough time before the door shut, to see into the office, see the professor behind his desk, and see him buckling and then zipping up his pants. That poor girl—those poor girls, had been Laura's thoughts as she had hurried out the unfamiliar exit.

She had felt anger for the girls and at seeing the man, but what she'd felt most was guilt over not having done something when she knew what was going on in there. Not that she had proof, it was just her gut and the fact that she had seen him adjusting his own clothes, as the girls had done. Without any corroborating statements, what did she really have? *Nothing.*

She had seen the professor, but he had not seen her, she was sure of it, but on the walk home, she'd had the unnerving sense that someone was watching her, following her. At home, she had thanked her babysitter/landlord, then had locked up as she normally did. But in the morning, as she had opened the door for Gwen to leave, she'd been alarmed to find it unlocked. She'd had a restless sleep and figured she would have heard someone come in if that were the case, but then she'd also been positive she had locked and latched the door.

At work, she'd been surprised to find a little celebration set up for her in the back bakery area, the owners had put up a small banner with the words *Congratulations* on it, and blew plastic horns and had applauded her for completing her course, then they'd announced they were making her manager and giving her a raise to boot.

She had been so appreciative for everything they'd done for her that the unease she'd felt earlier had begun to dissipate, but it had swiftly returned when she'd been out back writing up orders for supplies and had heard the radio spew out the morning news, *"The Professor of International Business, at the renowned Notre Dame of Maryland University, was found dead this morning."*

She had expected to see a new postcard that week, but by the end of April and on into June, Laura had still not received one.

She had wanted so badly to stay; she had a great job, a comfortable home, and even Gwen had been doing well with attending school in junior kindergarten. Had she gotten too comfortable and left the door unlocked, she wondered? She hadn't been keeping up with her usual surveillance of her surroundings, but with work, school and Gwen, she'd been too exhausted to perform her usual list of keep-safe tasks.

Come the end of June, she had been full on back to her compulsive checking of the security hardware she had put in place, and making mental notes on any new people she saw at the bakery or near the house.

Two years passed, and there had been no other murders reported, and little news about the serial killer, other than a short broadcast on how it had been two years now since the last killing, yet Laura had still kept up with her safety routine. Gwen had become less and less impressed with the restrictions Laura had imposed on her, but shortly after Gwen's 7th birthday, when fatefully another postcard arrived, it was clear to Laura by the message, that the time had come again to move.

The message read,

> You have overstayed your welcome, Laura.
> I killed that professor for you, yet you stayed this time.
> You've gotten too comfortable now, and if you contact the police, you and your daughter will NOT live to regret it.
> Don't ever forget, I'm watching you both.
> It's time for you to leave.

Laura had their escape packing down to a science, along with all her regular safety tasks she'd been doing over the past year, and this time she had been even better prepared for this inevitable move.

She had gotten letters of reference from her bosses and one from her landlord in advance, just in case, plus she had her college certificate for the business course she'd taken, and she'd had a story prepared for her landlord and her bosses at the bakery. She had written them both letters stating that she had been urgently requested back to her hometown to attend to her ailing parents. In the letters, she'd also expressed her sincere regret for leaving them so suddenly, which was painfully truer than her story she'd given for leaving them.

Laura had their belongings packed and hadn't hesitated to move again, and that's how they'd ended up in Charlottesville, Virginia. And though it had been six years and six moves since Laura started this trek across the country, aiming to escape the obsessive eyes of this serial killer, her time in Charlottesville had proven beneficial. As a result of Laura's extensive involvement in the family-built chain-bakery, two weeks ago she'd been asked to go work for another family member, to help them get a new location up and running, in North Carolina. And for the first time, Laura would be moving for the right reason, opportunity, and not out of fear.

Chapter 6

Monday, July 8, 2019 – Royal Oak, MI

Gwen and Scott live in an eight-unit, three floor walk-up apartment building built in 1920. It was old for sure, but it had lots of charm and it was close to everything they needed.

Scott had told Gwen about the vacant apartment when she had first been looking during her school orientation week. She had been bunking with a house full of girls in a sublet for about a month when Scott had seen her scanning the rental board in the student support area on campus. The girls had been nice, but it just wasn't the environment for her, and she'd been searching for a small space of her own. She hadn't been looking for luxury, not with her savings and having to work part-time, but with Scott's help, she'd landed the cute studio which was about 650 sq. ft. with the kitchen and bathroom on one side and the living room space with a large window that started at about waist-height on the far wall. Gwen had had to set up her television in front of the window partially blocking the view out. Her three-seater pull-out-bed couch divided the kitchen and living room facing the television and window. The door into the apartment was on the right in the center of the wall and next to the kitchen space. And along the left-hand-side wall of the small space was a series of built-in closets for clothing and storage. It was an efficient space and exactly what Gwen had needed. Any more space would have been a waste in her mind. Scott's place, a one-bedroom, on the same floor as Gwen's, wasn't much bigger at 810 sq. ft., and the building was only a 6-minute walk to the train station and a 2-minute walk to the coffee shop.

She and Scott worked most shifts together, which was great for Gwen since she could hitch a ride with him, but for anything else, like going to see her mother or heading anywhere for that matter, it was the people mover Amtrak that she would have to take. It was about an hour train ride to get to Gwen's mother's place, and she knew she should visit more but things had been super busy with her last month of training.

"What's with the paper flowers?" Scott asked, sitting down on the couch, examining the colourful homemade floral arrangement on Gwen's side table next to the couch. He was wearing his usual gym-gear and been heading to the gym clearly, but he had popped over for a quick visit this morning and had proceeded to eat half the toast she'd made for herself.

Gwen crossed from the living rooms space to the kitchen to put her breakfast dishes in the sink. "Long story short, we moved a lot when I was a kid and my mother used to get me one of those pads with the multi-coloured construction papers in it, and we'd make a paper garden on the wall of my bedroom. We never really had any art on the walls other than the cheap pieces that came as part of the furnished apartments we had lived in. It was the same with Christmas and Halloween, we made homemade decorations out of paper. When you moved as much as we did, hauling holiday decorations from place to place just wasn't doable. Other than those holidays, we never really celebrated much else with just the two of us." She sipped the last of her already cold coffee.

"What about birthdays?" he asked, trying to arrange the paper flowers, and failing.

"Oh, birthdays were different. My mother and I share the same birthday month just a week apart, so we always did something special. We still made homemade party hats, but she would get balloons and streamers from one of those stores where everything is a buck or less. Money was tight, but she made it special. She said that birthdays weren't a big thing when she was growing up, so she wanted me to remember mine as wonderful times in my life." Gwen felt a small pull of a smile at the corner of her mouth, as a few of those memories circled her thoughts.

"Well, I bet you had some amazing cakes, with her being a baker and all," Scott said, standing and giving his stomach a rub.

"Ha, ya, well... I'm not much into sweets, so cake wasn't big on my list of birthday wants."

"No cake—are you insane?" Scott said, chuckling and shaking his head.

"Don't forget I worked at the bakery weekends all through high school. My favorite thing was the jalapeno cheddar bread — still is, never any of the pastries. That made into a grilled cheese paired with a homemade tomato soup—is the best thing ever. My mother always keeps a couple loaves in the freezers for just such an occasion."

"Man, that sounds excellent. Maybe I should go visit your mom for you." He passed a hand across the back of his neck and strode into the small kitchen space.

"Wait, I lied. The only sweets I will eat are the chocolate chip cookies she makes—she uses M&Ms instead of chips. She keeps those in the freezer too. You can nuke them in the microwave, and they come out all warm and chewy." She took in a breath through her nose at the scented memory of it.

"Yer killing me, here, Gwen." He rubbed his stomach again and then opened her fridge.

She laughed. "I have to go visit Mom today, told her I'd be over for lunch. I'll try to remember to bring some cookies home with me. I'm the only one who eats them, so she won't mind," she said, zipping up her knapsack.

"It's about time you went to see her," he said, shutting the door then.

"I know-I know. She's been bugging me to go visit. Plus, I want to go through this old trunk she has. I haven't rifled through it in years, not since we first moved to Ann Arbor. From what I remember, Mom had a bunch of old textbooks, so maybe she has a yearbook or two."

"I'm heading out—need a ride to the station?" Scott said, as he headed for the door to her apartment.

"Sure—I'll take it," Gwen said, despite it only being a short walk. She grabbed up her knapsack then and followed him to the door.

An hour later, the train from Royal Oak was pulling into the Ann Arbor station, and from there it was also just a short walk to her mother's place.

At the front door to the garden home, Gwen gave the door the special *it's me Gwen* knock to let her Mom know she was here, then she unlocked the door with her key. It had been a security habit they had created for themselves, and well, old habits die hard.

"Hello, Dolly!" she heard her mother call out. Her mother had named her after a Canadian author, Gwendolyn MacEwen. She had told Gwen that the first name had stuck with her after reading one of the poems written by the author about childhood. But the nickname, *Dolly*, had been one of those *stranger danger*— secret code things they had developed, and an old habit her mother still used that Gwen wished *had* died.

"It's Gwen, mom!" she called back as she walked from the hall to the open-concept kitchen-dining-living room space.

She found her mother in the kitchen area making—what else, a grilled cheese sandwich, and there was a pot of homemade tomato soup warming on the stove. "It smells amazing in here," Gwen said. Wrapping an arm around her mother who was flipping the grilled cheesy goodness.

"Just in time," her mother said, reaching into the cupboard for a plate and two bowls. "It's about time you came to see your old mum too."

"Hey—I called you last week. You went out of town remember?" Gwen set her knapsack on the floor next to the dining table.

"Yes, about that." She ladled the soup into the bowls, then used the spatula to shift the sandwich from the pan onto the plate. "Here, sit down. Eat." Her mother set the bowls and then the plate with the sandwich on the dining table.

"You said your mom was sick. Is she okay"? Gwen asked, before blowing on the soup she had scooped up in her spoon.

Her mother sighed. "No… she's not… she passed, actually— but she had been extremely ill, and had been for some time I was told. It had just been a matter of time. She had all her affairs in order. Probably a blessing, no one should have to live like that."

"Sorry, Mom" Gwen said, giving her mother's hand a little squeeze. She knew her mother and her grandmother had been estranged, but it was her mom after all. She couldn't imagine what it would be like to lose her own mother. "Are you okay?"

"Oh—yes, I'm fine, yes. Everything had already been arranged it seemed, I just had to take care of some paperwork and it was why they had needed me there. I'm not sure I would have gone otherwise." She pulled out the chair next to Gwen and sat down.

"I'm glad you are okay, and I'm sorry you had to go deal with all that," Gwen said. Gwen hadn't been all that interested in her mother's past before, plus her mother had never enjoyed talking about it, and it made for a sour topic. Gwen's mother had not spoken to her own mother in years. She had shared that with Gwen when she was young and had first asked about family. Her mother's father was dead, he had died just after her mother had graduated high school, that much Gwen knew. Her mother had given her little else about them, other than the name of the town her mother had lived in as a child. Gwen had asked about her own father, but again she hadn't been given much. Only that he had also died, and that he and her mom had been married only a few days before he'd been killed in a car crash. His name was Frank, her mother had told her, but Gwen had never seen a picture of him or her grandparents. "I don't suppose you have any of those amazing M&M cookies in the freezer?" Gwen asked, shifting the topic, knowing there was always cookies in the freezer.

"Did you want me to make a care package for you?" she said, getting up from the table, and grabbing up both of their now empty bowls. She grinned over her shoulder at Gwen as she rinsed out the bowls in the sink.

"Better pack extra. I told Scott about your famous cookies," she said, taking the last bite of her sandwich before getting up and crossing to the sink. She ran the plate under the running water and set it next to the bowls. "I'll wash these — don't touch them, but I just want to check something first. Be right back," Gwen said, then she rushed upstairs to her old bedroom.

But instead of heading into her old room, she went to her mother's room, to the walk-in closet to be more precise. She had wanted to check the contents of the old trunk for any old yearbooks, check to see if Detective Franklin had attended the same high school. He had said he was older than her mother, but they could have still been at the same school. Either way, she had also wanted to see if there were any photos in the yearbooks of her mother from when she was young.

At the back of the closet she found the trunk, a battered and beaten thing now from being dragged with them each time they had moved. Gwen knelt in front of the trunk.

Inside she found several stacks of books. The first stack were textbooks, the top four on the pile were, Gardner's Art Through the Ages, Computer Science Illuminated, Comparative literature: A Critical Introduction, and Living Language Complete Edition. There were a few novels in the next pile, but the others were mainly textbooks, those she'd seen before and from courses her mother had taken over the years, Gwen had assumed, but there were no yearbooks in the lot. Under the last textbook, one titled Understanding the Classic American Novel, she was surprised to find a stack of letters. Both this textbook and these letters she had not seen before.

"What are you doing?" Gwen's mother asked, startling her, standing now in the closet's entrance.

"Looking for old yearbooks or photos from when you were young," Gwen said, shifting the textbooks back into piles.

"I don't have any," her mother said, leaning against the jamb of the closet door.

"Why do you keep all these textbooks?" Gwen asked, standing then.

"Oh, I don't know—I like to learn, never got to go to college full time, you know that. Get out of there now," her mother said, appearing a bit flustered, shooing her out of the closet and then out of the bedroom. "Come tell me about how your on-the-job-training is going." She gave Gwen a light tap on the elbow to go down the stairs ahead of her.

"Well, I was on scene at that murder the other week—the one linked to the serial killer," Gwen tossed out, before reaching the first floor. She turned back to see her mother stopped in the middle of the staircase. "Mom?"

"Sorry, dear... yes, the one in the news," her mother said, quickly descending the last few stairs. "You didn't have to see the dead body, did you?"

"Mom, I've seen a dead body. It's sort of part of the job," Gwen said, standing next to the dining table.

"Yes, okay—I see," her mother said, going to the kitchen window and pushing back the curtain to look out.

"Do you remember hearing about the very first murder? It happened not far from where you grew up, in Hanover."

"No... I don't recall," she said, moving across to the living room to peek out the window there.

"The detective working the case is from your hometown. Did you ever know a Jim Franklin?"

She heard her mother take in a sharp breath. Then she turned and said, "I'm just going to go for a walk. You'll lock up won't you dear?"

"Mom, are you... okay?" Gwen had started to ask, as her mother grabbed up her satchel from the hall table, but she had been out the door before Gwen could finish.

Chapter 7

Laura - July 8th, 2019 - Ann Arbor, MI

Hearing that Gwen had been on the scene at that latest murder had thrown Laura for a loop. Thoroughly on edge, she had struggled to get air into her lungs and had rushed out before letting her daughter see her in such a state. She knew she was going to have to tell her daughter eventually, about what she knew about the murders, about the stalker, the man who had been chasing her across the country. In hopes to calm her nerves now, she had walked the five blocks to the local university campus to further walk the grounds.

Six years and she'd not heard a peep, then the other week as she'd been working in the back of the bakery, the news had spewed out from the small television, informing her that based on the MO, the killer was back. Not in her town, but close enough—too close in fact, as the murder had been on the campus her daughter had attended. Why was he back and why now, she had wondered and worried?

She had been in Ann Arbor now since the fall of 2013, and it had been halfway through her daughter's sophomore year in high school, when Gwen had begged her to stay here. She had told Gwen that she would think about it. And though there had been no postcard received on this move, there had been on the four moves prior.

After two years in Virginia, Gwen had established some nice friendships, so she had not been impressed with them moving to North Carolina. They had stayed there for two years while Laura had been running the company's catering expansion. There had been no message from the killer, nor had she heard of any new murders. Well, not until that June, when the professor of Engineering who had been visiting the local University, had wound up dead. When a postcard arrived in July they had packed up and moved to West Virginia, but come that September, there had been yet another murder, another Professor killed at the local University.

When another postcard arrived the following January, they were on the move again, this time to Gambier, Ohio. And the only reason they had stopped there was because Gwen had been experiencing severe abdominal pains. The doctor in the emergency, had kept saying it was all in Gwen's head, had even called for someone in psych to evaluate her. To pay for the medical bills, they had had to stay in the town so Laura could find work.

Then the day of Gwen's 13th birthday they had been back to the hospital with her once again suffering abdominal pains. The same doctor had been there, but luckily for them, there was another doctor in charge, and he'd examined Gwen this time. Laura had known Gwen's pain had not been in her head, and the new doctor had proven such, and had diagnosed her with an irritable bowel, that was potentially brought on by stress. Talk about guilt, Laura knew she was to blame for the stress, and for the instability with making her daughter move all the time.

The following day at her waitress job, the best she could find under the circumstances, the public TV they had on the wall of the diner, had shown a news report about the Professor of Psychology from the local college being killed, and there had been a photo with the broadcast. The photo was of the doctor, the first one who had seen Gwen, the one who had said the pain was all in her head, who had also been a professor at the university. A few weeks later in May, a postcard arrived, and Laura had gotten her daughter and herself out of that town as fast as she could, moving them to Indiana.

It would be another two years before a news bulletin provided the horrifying update that another professor had been killed, this time a Professor of Film Studies from the local university. A week later another postcard had followed, and it had been time to move again. In July of 2013 Laura had landed them in Charleston, Illinois.

Stressful moves had been the understatement at that point, so in hopes of easing the stress and tension with her daughter, and to perhaps educate them both, Laura had suggested she and Gwen take a summer course in nutrition at the university, to better understand Gwen's stomach condition and how it was impacted by food. Gwen had been open, and it had helped heal their frayed relationship some.

Then on the last day of the course, when another teacher, the Professor of Exercise Science, had overheard the reason why they'd taken the course, he had gone off on a rant, telling them what Gwen should and shouldn't eat, all geared to sports nutrition, and the opposite to what they'd learned, both from the doctor who had diagnosed her and from on the course. The professor had said, *"The doctors don't know what they are talking about."* He'd been pushy and basically a jerk, and… had ended up dead. So much for being healthy if someone kills you, Laura had morbidly thought. When Laura had seen the death on the news, it had been paired with an update on the lead detective running the case. The news had stated that with the latest killings being somewhat back-to-back, that the detective had turned his focus on tracking the serial killer *West* across the country. That had also been when it had dawned on Laura, that she needed to change her travel route, backtrack or something, go North to Michigan, maybe. And when yet another postcard showed up, they were on the move, again.

After they had first arrived in Ann Arbor, Laura had done her usual security routine, but this time she had added reinforcement to her entry door buy installing a door strike plate. She'd been told by the guy at the local hardware store that it helped to strengthen the door's weak spot, the jamb, by providing a heavy-duty plate and extra-long screws needed to withstand a burglar trying to kick in the door. The guy had said, *"Depending on when the dead bolt was installed, if it hadn't been in the last 10 years, it would need to be reinforced."* Then he had pointed her in the direction of the hardware she would need and gave her the instructions on how to install it.

Her front door may have been reinforced now, but the internal struggle she had about all the moving and the lying to her daughter had weakened her resolve. So, when Gwen had asked about staying, Laura had decided to do a little research on another topic to help with her decision. At the library in town, she had looked up *stalking* and had found several psychology magazines and some self-help resources.

The first magazine she'd found had an article that defined stalking as repeated and unwanted attention, harassment, contact, or any other behavior directed at a specific person that would cause a reasonable person to feel fear. It cited a 2006, large-scale representative study of stalking behavior across three continents. In it the report stated that 2–13% of males and 8–32% of females are victimized by stalking at some point in their adult lives, and in most cases, the person is stalked by someone they know. It went on to say that the relentless neurotic nature of the stalker can be anything from harassing their targets, calling them repeatedly, to even sending letters and gifts. And if ineffective, the stalker may escalate to more intrusive behaviors like spying, and unpredictably confronting their victims. She could identify with that, but the part she had found useless, had been the part about how there was little to explain what exactly motivated a stalker, and the article had focused more on how to therapeutically treat these people.

Part of the article stated that most stalkers don't suffer from delusions or hallucinations, but many suffer from other forms of mental illness such as depression, substance abuse, and personality disorders. At the bottom of the write-up, there had been some guidelines for stalking victims, and it indicated that *if applied, they may reduce the odds of physical or emotional harm from their stalker*. All she had seen was the *'may'* part in that, and that had not been hugely helpful. She had been hoping to better understand what motivated a person to obsess over another person, or what delusions could possibly stir those feelings for another person to commit murder. She hadn't wanted that— hadn't asked for it, but it had happened, and she needed to know what she could do about it.

In the next magazine, an older one from 2000, there had been an article on a study conducted in 1993 by an Australian stalking expert, who was a clinical director and chief psychologist at a high-security hospital for mentally ill offenders, where he had analyzed the behavior of 145 diagnosed stalkers. He and his colleagues had defined five stalker subtypes to facilitate diagnosis and treatment.

Laura had made a photocopy of that article and had read it several times over when she had gotten home. But when Gwen had asked her then why they moved so much, Laura had not been ready to tell her the truth and had told her instead that she didn't like to stay in one place too long and that she was looking for the perfect place for them. And that had been when her daughter had said, *"Ann Arbor is the perfect place, Mom."*

In the end, she had made the decision to stay, obviously, but how was she going to protect herself, protect her daughter, she had agonized then? Laura glanced down at her purse. She hadn't wanted to get a gun, hadn't wanted one around her daughter, so instead she had opted to purchase and keep pepper spray with her at all times now. As Laura strolled further through the campus, she patted the side of her purse and then adjusted the strap at her shoulder.

It wasn't a purse per se, it was an RAF blue canvas travel shoulder messenger satchel, that she'd gotten at the local army surplus store, and had had since before Gwen was born. In high school, she had put several colourful pin-buttons on it. Over time she had removed some, the ones that had stopped having meaning or impact as she had gotten older. She'd had one from the local library from her hometown, that had been the first to come off, as it gave away where she might have been from. The one with 'When it Rains it Poes', a play on the name of one of her favorite authors, had been the next to come off. The rainbow, flower-power and peace happy face had been the one to come off after that, mainly because it felt juvenile and she had wanted to be seen as an adult. The last one she had removed had been the one with the words 'The Twilight Zone', referring to the original, and was considered vintage, though she'd never seen the tv show. Her daughter had given her a button from her high school when she'd gotten to stay in Ann Arbor, and then she'd replaced it a few weeks ago, in salute of her upcoming graduation from college with one that had the words 'Parent of a First Responder' on it. Laura wore it proudly, and she had followed it up by putting a new peace sign happy face one on as well. Peace and happiness, Laura thought as she brushed a finger across the two pins left on her purse.

It had been six years since the killer disappeared. And in that time Laura had built a nice life for herself and her daughter, though Gwen wasn't living at home anymore and was living an hour away in a different city. Gwen had left right after high school, gotten a job working at the college she been attending, in the cafeteria. She'd worked part-time with Laura at the bakery during high school. *"Saving for college,"* she would say to Laura. It had taken Gwen longer than normal to complete her training to be a paramedic because of her having to work to pay for things. Laura always felt guilty for that, had felt guilty for a lot of things. She had raised her daughter to be independent, but the last thing Laura had wanted was for her to move out.

In Ann Arbor, with all the reference letters Laura had gathered, she had been able to get a house to rent instead of an apartment. It was a garden home and for the first time she had chosen to live in a community-style housing development, figuring that maybe more eyes on them meant more security, the busybodies could be good surveillance people without realizing they were. It seemed to work too. No one got anywhere near their house or meandered around the community grounds without a neighbor reporting it or confronting the person, and Laura loved that. She couldn't blame Gwen for wanting to move out though, they'd shared so many spaces together, and Gwen had needed a space of her own. Laura was loving her job here too, helping to run the bakery. She had introduced them to the catering option as well, and it had become highly lucrative for the bakery.

She and her daughter had both flourished in these past few years living in Michigan. Laura had watched her daughter grow into a smart, capable, young woman. She had been there to watch her daughter get her driver's license, though Laura still didn't own a car, she didn't even have her own driver's license. But she did have a cell phone, had gotten one shortly after moving here, mainly because it was added security, giving her and her daughter a way to communicate, for emergencies Laura had told herself. She only had three numbers in her contact list: Gwen, the bakery, and Marlene, her friend—her only friend.

She had met Marlene just before Gwen's high school graduation, when Laura had been out on a break from the bakery, sitting and enjoying her coffee with one of the pastries she'd made that morning. She had been hesitant initially when Marlene had first approached her, sitting on the bench herself for a break. She had been friendly, commenting about the weather, but before Laura had realized it, they had been full on discussing the feelings Laura had been having about the upcoming graduation. They had ended their first conversation on a happy note, when Laura had told her how much she loved it here, where she lived, her job, and even her neighbors.

The following week when Laura had gone for her break again, Marlene had been sitting on the bench when she had gotten there. To Laura's delight, their conversation continued as did their friendship. Now they meet every Tuesday like clockwork and over the past three years they have discussed a variety of topics. It was the perfect spot, up the street from the bakery and just up the street from the college where Marlene was a professor of psychology. Laura had begun to trust Marlene and had taken comfort in the consistency of their meetups. Laura had liked where she was, liked this little town and the people here, but it had been traumatic when Gwen had left for a college out of town, so it had been wonderful to have someone to talk to about the empty nest stuff.

Gwen was graduating from college in less than a month, and she had wanted to talk to Marlene about it, but having been away last week, she hadn't been able to meet with her. Laura had often wondered if she would ever finally trust someone enough to tell them what she had been dealing with over the past 20 years.

The killer was back… tomorrow was Tuesday… and she would see Marlene back at their bench. So, maybe then would be a good time to tell her friend the story, Laura thought, as she turned and headed back toward her home.

Chapter 8

Last week had been the first time in the past three years since Laura and Marlene had become friends, that they hadn't met for coffee and pastries. Laura had been so anxious since yesterday to speak with her, that she'd asked the other baker to cover for her, so she could take some extra time for her break, and had headed to the bench early, mainly to calm her nerves. She had finally been feeling ready to tell her friend everything.

Laura already knew a lot about her friend, Marlene had shared things about her life easily, and everything Laura had learned about her friend she had appreciated, and as their friendship had grown, Laura had found she liked basically everything about Marlene. They were the same age, which was nice as they related to a lot of the same things, though there was a lot that Laura also struggled to connect with, yet she always found those topics and the dialog about them particularly interesting. Laura had realized her growth had been in the struggling and she had always enjoyed learning.

"Heeey, I missed you last week," Laura heard a woman's voice say, and she turned towards the voice to see Marlene strolling over to the bench with an extra-large coffee in hand.

Laura waved. "Hey, stranger."

Marlene was wearing a black dress, her typical attire which was usually either a long flowy skirt or dress, in one of her favorite colours, black, navy, or dark brown, and at a length that went to her ankles. She was tall like Laura, taller in fact, and probably 6′ 3″ with the high heeled shoes and boots she insisted on wearing. Laura never wore heels; in fact, she rarely ever wore a dress. She was most comfortable in her jeans and t-shirts or baker attire. They'd had a good chuckle though about how men often find tall women intimidating, and how Marlene had upped her game by wearing a minimum three-inch heel, even in the summer she wore platform sandals. But body-wise that was where the similarities between the two of them ended. Laura may have been tall, but she was slim where Marlene was heftier, more like a female athlete with a little bit extra around the middle. With her size you would have thought she would have come off as intimidating, but she had a pleasant happy face and full cheeks that bunched when she smiled. Her eyes were big and bright, a light green colour, and she wore her pale blond hair pulled back in a bun similar to how Laura wore hers, though Laura's hair was a dark strawberry blond similar to Gwen's. Her voice had almost a musical quality to it and she had a soft laugh, more like a giggle, and not what you would expect from a woman of her stature.

"Family stuff—had to go see my mother," Laura said, when Marlene got closer.

"Your mother—why didn't you tell me?" Marlene asked, a lilt of surprise in her voice.

"It was a quick trip," she said, making room for Marlene on the bench. Whoever got there first usually sat in the middle to save space for the other and just in case someone else came along and chose to sit down.

"She okay?" Marlene asked, sitting and taking up the rest of the space by setting her purse next to her on the bench. "You never talk about her."

Laura took in a deep breath. "She passed, actually," Laura said, letting out the breath. "She wasn't well—but I'm fine. We hadn't spoken in years. Not since Gwen was born in fact." She forced a smile. "Married young, new baby, dead husband—she had been pretty judgmental about it. Even blamed me for my father's death—said my leaving had killed him. It's why I'd stayed away as long as I had," Laura explained, then handed her friend the *Kanelbulle* she always brought for Marlene. It was Laura's version of a Swedish cinnamon roll. Marlene had said they reminded her of her childhood because her mother used to make them and had tried to teach her, but had failed, not because she hadn't been a good teacher, Marlene had just been more interested in the eating than the baking.

"Oh, thank you-thank you," Marlene said, snatching up the goodie bag. "No one escapes family drama, I'm sorry to say, but I am sorry you had to deal with that level of it, and I'm sorry your mother died and you had to deal with that too." She gave Laura's forearm a light squeeze.

Changing the subject, Laura asked, "Did you see your parents on Sunday?" Marlene's parents lived nearby and still lived in the same house Marlene had grown up in. She had told Laura the house had lots of room for gatherings and family visits, and she did Sunday dinners with them most weekends. Laura had felt envious of this, not having any siblings of her own, nor had she had any large family gatherings to speak of.

"Yes, and my brothers showed up with their spouses and all the grandkids in tow." She grinned, then sipped her coffee. Marlene was a first generation American, but her parents were both from Sweden. She was the youngest of four, and all born right here in Ann Arbor. The three older siblings, all boys, were all in the medical field and were bigwigs in the Detroit medical community.

"That sounds nice," Laura said, giving a sarcastic grin back to her friend.

"Don't get me wrong, I love my brothers and their families, but I think they all would like me to be married with kids too. My parents know I love my life the way it is, and they have plenty of grandkids to keep them busy. But being the only daughter—you know the drill." She bit into her pastry and chewed. Then she said, "I really do love my life. I like being single, though I do date—nothing serious, you know. I'm not looking for anything serious, I get enough of that with my job." She took another bite.

"I understand," Laura said, she felt the same about her life, but she had *no* interest in dating. Well, she had felt the same about her life up until the other week, when she had heard the news about the killer being back.

"Hey, we should go out sometime—maybe we could celebrate Gwen's graduation, I'd love to meet her," Marlene said, cutting into Laura's morbid musings.

"I'd love for you to meet Gwen," Laura said, forcing a smile and then sipping her coffee.

"We've been meeting like this for years—I know we have differing schedules, but we should be able to find time for a girl's night—just the two of us. I know a great restaurant-bar. Then we can make time for a get-together with Gwen nearer to the end of the month," Marlene added, pulling her cell phone from her purse. "Let me check my schedule."

Laura set her coffee down on the bench and then removed her own cell phone from her purse. "I'll check my shifts for the coming weeks."

"Ooohh, look at you with your calendar app—fancy," Marlene teased. She had helped Laura set it up last year to help her keep track of not just her schedule but also Gwen's.

"Har-har," Laura said, grinning proudly while she scanned her digital calendar. "How about, Saturday—we could meet for lunch."

"Ah, ya—no, I have a client this Saturday around noon," Marlene said.

"Client?" Laura asked, mild confusion setting in. Laura slid her phone back into her purse.

"Yes, I don't normally see patients on weekends, but this is a special case," Marlene said, adding to Laura's now growing confusion.

"Patients?" Laura questioned, the reality of her confusion settling in. "Yer a shrink?"

"Well, yes—I thought you knew," Marlene said. "I have a small practice out of my house, but my cases aren't something I share with friends."

Laura knew she had a small two-story home, close enough to downtown to be social but far enough away that she didn't hear the noise of it. She had told Laura that much, but she had thought Marlene was a professor at the university. "How did I not know this? I thought you just taught psychology." Laura wrung the strap of her purse with both hands.

"Yes, I do that too, but I only lecture on Tuesday and it's one class, and it's why I'm able to meet here. It's good for me to get out and I like the campus and the people-watching. I don't schedule sessions on Tuesdays for that reason."

"I guess I just assumed you had a whole curriculum, not just one lecture." Laura stood then, her gut screaming not to trust Marlene. But she *had* trusted her. "I'm sorry, I can't stay," she said, checking her watch. "I forgot I need to get something for Gwen on my break." It was a lie, and a knee jerk reaction, Laura knew it, but the anxiety she was feeling over not knowing this about Marlene after all this time, had critically disturbed her rational thinking.

"Laura?" she heard Marlene call after her as she took off up the street. But Laura did not look back.

Chapter 9

The following week on Tuesday, at the regular time they normally met, Laura headed out to the bench in hopes of finding Marlene there. She needed to apologize for running off like she had.

Laura had wanted to call Marlene, she should have called, but instead, Laura had spent most of her spare time educating and focusing herself on the topics of *trust* and *safety*. She had done this to help her get past the anxiety she had experienced over not knowing about Marlene being a psychologist. Trust, the noun, is defined *as reliance on the integrity, strength, ability, surety, etc., of a person or thing, and confidence, confident expectation of something or hope*. The verb trust is defined as *relying upon or place confidence in someone or something and to trust in another's honesty*. And safety, was defined as *the state of being safe; freedom from the occurrence or risk of injury, danger, or loss*. Marlene hadn't lied to her, she'd only made the assumption that Laura already knew, and Laura had made the wrong assumption that Marlene only taught classes in psychology.

All that focus on trust and safety that Laura had done, didn't seem to matter now she realized, because Marlene *was* at the bench as she had hoped, but she wasn't sitting alone… she was sitting on their bench, with a man.

Laura didn't know many men in town, many men in general for that matter, and she certainly didn't recognize this guy.

"Oh, hiii," Marlene said, when Laura approached the bench. "Laura, this is Professor Christian Weick. He just moved into town, and he's working with me at the college."

"Hi—nice to meet you," the man said, not bothering to get up or make room on the bench. Not that Laura wanted to sit near him. "Dr. Branden mentioned she meets you here Tuesdays after her class."

"Hi," Laura said, though sensing the need to run off again.

"How was your week?" Marlene asked, her usual rosy cheeks bunching in a smile.

"Here," Laura said, handing Marlene her pastry, her eyes still on the bench. "I can't stay, just wanted to say hi—busy day at the bakery," she lied, pointing back down the street towards her work. She winced, realizing she had just shared where she worked with this stranger.

"Christian—you should really go check out the amazing delights at the bakery. Laura here is a wizard with the pastry bag," Marlene said, promoting Laura's skill when it didn't need the attention.

"Gotta go—sorry," Laura said, turning then to head back the way she had come.

She had heard them both call their goodbyes, but she had just kept walking. She'd only just learned that her friend of three years was a shrink, then when she'd worked through her issues over it, her friend shows up at their usual spot to meet—not with her, but with some guy. This was *their* time to talk, not a time for socializing with others.

Back at the bakery, Laura headed for the office. She still had some time on her break, so she went on the company computer to do a google search on this Professor what's-his-name, Christian Weick.

She'd typed his name in with and without the 'professor' title, and after paging through whatever she could find on anyone with that name, she had come up with nothing, well, nothing other than the long list of professional accolades she had found referencing his many contributions to the psychology field, along with his numerous achievements and degrees.

What was the matter with her? Marlene was her friend; they had been friends for over three years now. Why was she letting all these insignificant things get to her? So-what if she was a psychologist, and so what if she was chatting with a colleague on their bench. The bench didn't belong to them, they just used it for their meet-ups, the bench belonged to the city and they'd been lucky to use it, she'd been lucky to find a friend like Marlene. But then why was she being so paranoid?

She googled *paranoia*.

The online dictionary showed the definition as, *a mental condition characterized by delusions of persecution, unwarranted jealousy, or exaggerated self-importance, typically elaborated into an organized system*. The psychiatry website she brought up next, had it defined as, *a mental disorder characterized by systematized delusions and the projection of personal conflicts, which are ascribed to the supposed hostility of others, sometimes progressing to disturbances of consciousness and aggressive acts believed to be performed in self-defense or as a mission*. But on the same website, she found a description she preferred, that read, *a baseless or excessive suspicion of the motives of others*. That was her alright. She wasn't paranoid, really, she was just an idiot who had been running scared too long. Now, she owed Marlene two apologies.

When Laura finished her break, she went out to the front area of the bakery where she found… her friend Marlene… standing near the entrance to the bakery. "I just stopped in to see that you were okay," Marlene said, when she noticed Laura come out from the back.

"I'm fine—really. I'm sorry for being so unfriendly to your colleague—for rushing off, and for cutting our time short last week." Laura's shoulders slumped. "I've just had a lot on my mind with Gwen's graduation and I guess I just really needed to talk to you today." It wasn't a lie, she did have a lot on her mind, but it was way more than just her daughter's graduation. Laura came closer through the space between the display case and the counter, to make the conversation more private. Not that there was a lot of privacy in a public bakery.

Marlene shook her head. "I'm sorry—I know Tuesdays is *our* time, and we haven't gotten to see each other much. So, I'm sorry—I should have touched base with Professor Weick after our chat time." Marlene gave Laura a faint smile, then reached out and drew a hand down Laura's sleeve, giving it a shake at the wrist.

Laura felt the sincerity in both Marlene's words and her actions for coming to check on her, and she smiled back at her friend. She liked that Marlene had come looking for her, that she had realized what Laura's non-verbal attitude at the bench had truly meant. And feeling more confident now, Laura said, "We should meet up—tonight. Maybe go to that restaurant you mentioned last week."

"Yes—I'd love that," Marlene said, her smile widening.

"Me too," Laura said, grinning again.

Marlene put one hand on her hip and checked the time on her cell phone in her other hand. "How about tonight—say 7ish?" she suggested.

"Perfect, that will give me time to change after work," Laura said.

"I'll text you the name and address," Marlene said. "I better leave before I order something. Need to save my appetite for tonight."

Marlene winked, and it made Laura laugh. "Tonight, then," Laura said, through another chuckle.

"Tonight—see you there," Marlene confirmed, before turning and heading out the door.

"Nice friend you got there," the teenage girl at the cash counter said, "She was in the other week as well—when you were gone, asking about you."

Laura nodded. It was nice knowing someone cared about her whereabouts, cared about *her* for a change, she mused, as she headed back into the baking area.

When Laura's shift ended at 5 p.m. she hustled herself off home to get ready for her first girl's night out. She had just enough time to shower and change into something nice. She didn't have many good clothes and really the only nice thing she owned was the dress she'd bought to wear for Gwen's high school graduation. It still fit, luckily, even if it was a few years out of fashion. She didn't own any makeup, so the only change she could make to herself was with her hair. She normally wore it pulled back and in a tight bun, but after her shower she'd blown it dry, and since she preferred her hair off her face, she'd fastened the long length into a soft French braid.

Laura entered the restaurant to see the waving arms of Marlene who had found a nice bar-top table near the side windows. She was on time, but she'd had to swap her bag for the purse that went with her dress. She couldn't show up with that satchel of hers swung over her shoulder, but this purse wasn't big enough for her wallet and keys, cell phone and pepper spray, and she'd had to make a choice, and the pepper spray had lost out to needing money, communication and a way to lock her front door. When she had googled the restaurant's address on her phone, it had been further than she had realized, and she'd had to hoof it there. Thankfully, unlike Marlene, Laura only wore flats, making it easier to keep a brisk pace all the way. Laura ran a palm over her hair to smooth any strays that had escaped her hairdo, before shuffling over to the table.

"Did you drive?" Laura asked, maneuvering into the tall bar chair next to Marlene.

"No—I don't have a car, actually, don't need it. I'm like you—I walk everywhere," Marlene said, then leaned to one side and gestured to get the waitress's attention. "My parents have a car—only my mom drives, but I use it on occasion to go into Detroit, or drive them to family gatherings, my mom only drives in town." Marlene smiled. "We gather at least once a month at one of my brothers' homes—they take turns, and it's usually around someone's birthday. With a big group—it's easier to do birthday month." Marlene smiled and when the waitress stopped at their table.

"What can I get you, ladies?" The waitress asked, looking back and forth between the two of them.

"I'll have a Cosmo," Marlene said.

The waitress glanced at Laura.

"Uhmmm...," Laura began, unprepared to pick a drink.

"She'll have the same," Marlene told the girl. "They taste like Kool-Aid—you'll like it.

Laura had never had a Cosmo before, though she had tried Kool-Aid. Had made it for Gwen when she was a little girl, though Gwen hadn't liked it much, she hadn't been one for sweet things.

"Now about my practice," Marlene said, cutting to the chase.

Laura shook her head. "No—I understand, and I'm sorry about that. I reacted poorly—I'm deeply sorry," Laura said. She meant it, she wasn't upset about the whole 'client' thing anymore, in fact she had been hoping to get her professional opinion about her situation, about why someone would stalk her.

Marlene patted Laura's hand. "I really care about my patients, and I have a hard time not offering help to people in need," she said.

"Your advice to me over the years has made a huge difference in how I've dealt with the challenges in my life," Laura said, just as the waitress returned with their drinks.

When the waitress was gone, Marlene said, "It's my job to help others work through their conflicts, so I try to lead by example and make sure I talk about things bothering me etc., with a friend or colleague. Practice what I preach, ya know."

"Did you always want to be a psychologist?" Laura sniffed the drink.

Marlene tapped her glass against Laura's, then said, "Cheers," and took a sip. After swallowing, she said, "Well, I was following in my brothers' footsteps to become a doctor, I am a medical doctor, but I was more fascinated with the mind than the body, and chose to do my residency in psychology."

"I don't really drink," Laura admitted, lifting the fancy glass to take the tiniest of sips. "Mmm, it does taste like that kids' drink."

Marlene laughed. "I like a drink now and then, and usually like this, at a local restaurant or pub. I never drink alone—it's a social thing for me," she shared.

"Your job is stressful, I would imagine," Laura said, setting the glass back down.

"No—I don't really get stressed, but I guess if something is troubling me, I tend to eat my feelings. I'm human like the rest of the people on the planet."

"If you couldn't be a shrink, what else would you want to do for a living?" Laura asked, moving her glass further away from the edge of the table.

"Wow—that's a good question, I feel like you're examining me," Marlene said. "Kind of funny to be on the other side," she added, with a laugh.

Laura laughed too, and she was actually having a good time. She shouldn't have been so afraid, there was nothing to be scared about.

"What would I do if I couldn't do this job? I'd love to be a food critic, but I think you have to know about cooking," Marlene said. "That's more of a lark, but it would be fun—not eating the bad food—just the good stuff, yes?"

"Yes," Laura agreed, lifting her glass to take another tiny sip.

"What kind of music do you like," Marlene asked, when the music in the bar area got louder.

"Oh, I don't know," Laura said. She didn't know bands, or singers, though she liked when they had the radio on in the back bakery while they did their work. Her daughter had liked a variety of music, but she couldn't name any of it. "I like the oldies channel they have on at work." Laura took a glance around the bar area. It had begun to fill up since she had sat down. "You?" she asked, glancing back at Marlene.

"I like a lot of different genres, but I think anything I can dance to. Though it can be hard to find a partner willing to dance with me." Marlene laughed again.

Laura appreciated Marlene's sense of humor, though she tended to be self-deprecating yet nonapologetic about her size, she was the kind of person who knew her flaws and loved herself despite them. Laura envied her for that.

"I don't dance," Laura said, "but I am enjoying myself just sitting here." Laura clinked Marlene's glass with hers, then took another small sip.

Marlene's glass was empty now, and she was waving the waitress over again, giving her the peace-sign to indicate two more. She turned back then, and said, "I really enjoy people watching, must be the psychologist in me. People watching at a bar can be very entertaining." She raised her eyebrows a few times and grinned.

Laura scanned the room. There were even more people in the space now.

"Your daughter was athletic—played volleyball in high school, if I remember correctly," Marlene said, bringing Laura's attention back. "Did you play sports in high school?"

"Me, no—gawd no," Laura said, setting her drink down again.

"I tried volleyball—but it didn't keep my interest." Marlene shrugged. "People figured since I was tall that I'd love it, and I played my first year of high school, but that was it," Marlene said, as though she was embarrassed for failing at something.

The waitress stopped at their table with the drinks, exchanging Marlene's empty glass on the table with the full one from her tray, then placed the other full one next to Laura's still mostly full one.

"What was your most embarrassing moment in high school," Marlene asked, then took a long sip of her fresh drink.

"I don't think I have a most embarrassing moment—other than maybe right now for having nothing exciting to share," Laura said, feeling her face flush.

"Well, I've got one," Marlene said. "I punched a girl in high school once. She was making fun of me for being so tall—and I hadn't filled out yet." She motioned to her chest area. "But I could fight, having three older brothers n 'all. I had known better—but I had had enough."

Laura couldn't help it, she smiled.

"Broke her nose, mean girl—prom queen. I enjoyed it a little too much." Marlene let out a laugh. "I missed the prom because of it—but who cares."

Laura gasped out a laugh.

"Kids can be mean, being tall is not always great, and you find yourself needing to shrink yourself—and that's not good," Marlene added on a more serious note.

"What about your most embarrassing moment as an adult?" Laura asked, curiosity getting the best of her.

"Blind date—enough said," Marlene shot out, before taking a big gulp of her drink. They both laughed. Then Marlene leaned in and said, "Speaking of *not so* blind dates, that tall handsome guy at the end of the bar is checking you out."

Laura froze.

"Don't turn yet—I'll tell you when he looks away," Marlene said.

Laura figured this was typical banter and play between girlfriends but hearing that a man was staring at her didn't give her the girly goosebumps, it gave her the overwhelming need to pack up and run. "I'm not good with that," was all Laura could muster.

"Relax, he's coming over," Marlene said, leaning back from the table.

"Forgive me—but I can't do this," Laura said, as she shot out of her seat, then rushed across the room and out the front door.

Chapter 10

Laura was at the bench first this time, waiting for Marlene. She had done it again, taken off without explanation, though she had texted Marlene this time, on her way home from the restaurant, to say sorry for the rude exit she'd made, when she should have just explained herself, and had clarified that she had felt uncomfortable with that guy watching her. She had been so freaked out, she half expected to find a postcard under her door when she had gotten home. Marlene had written back saying not to worry, that she understood it was Laura's first time out in a long time. It had been Laura's first time out since before the birth of her daughter, but Marlene hadn't known that. Marlene had been so fun and outgoing that night, and Laura had been too embarrassed to tell her then, but they'd agreed to meet like usual at their regular spot to talk.

"Hey," Marlene said, when she approached the bench.

"Hey," Laura said, sensing her face redden, embarrassment surfacing.

Marlene sat down next to Laura, then turned to face her. "Is it me—am I too pushy?" Marlene asked. "I mean—I thought we were friends. You know you can tell me anything—anything that's bothering you too."

Was it possible to feel good and bad at the same time? She was so appreciative of Marlene for stating what she believed, that they were friends, but Laura felt anguished over the fact that she kept bolting out on her. "You have no idea how much our friendship means to me. It has been quite some time since I had someone to talk to—a girlfriend more importantly," Laura said, squeezing her hands together. "And I feel awful for how I've treated you, the childish way I keep running off without a reason. I mean I have reasons—maybe not great ones, but they feel valid in the moment. I'm so sorry." Laura looked down at her hands in her lap.

"Talk to me, Laura," Marlene said. Then she reached out and touched the top of Laura's hand.

"Okay… well… I'm not very good with men," Laura said, still looking down. "I've never had a boyfriend—other than Gwen's father, and well... he's the only man I've ever been with— *you know*." There was more that Laura needed to tell her friend, but she knew that she wasn't ready to share the details about the stalker, how it had affected her perception of men and that it was part of why she was struggling with, well, all of it.

"I don't know what it's like for you… to have found your true love—then lose him." Marlene patted Laura's hand, then pulled back.

Laura glanced up to face her friend.

"I thought I was in love once," Marlene shared then. "He was a friend of my oldest brother, but in retrospect now, I know it was mostly infatuation. And probably the closest I've come to love—romantic love." Marlene took in a deep breath, then sighed on the exhale. "Some may think being single is a problem—but I don't. My life has a wonderful flow and rhythm to it. I'm very happy with the way my life is," she added, smiling at Laura. "Tell me about your husband."

Laura gave her own heavy sigh. "He's dead."

"I know that, you told me—and I'm sorry for your loss," Marlene said.

"I appreciate your concern—really, I'd just prefer not to talk about it," Laura said. She didn't like talking about him, her father or men in general. She liked her life too, even though she missed Gwen terribly, and her life had been fairly tension-free for several years, up until a few weeks ago.

"My guess is you had a pretty strict upbringing—mine too," Marlene said, nodding, as if she had read Laura's thoughts. "Mine were strict but loving. I think with four kids, three being boys, that there needed to be some kind of order in the house. And they both worked too, so we all had responsibilities at home." Marlene tilted her head to the side, then added, "I respect them greatly and I don't envy them raising us, we were big kids to manage and had big mouths to feed." She giggled, and it made Laura laugh. Marlene's joy was contagious at times.

"I bet," Laura said, grinning over the image of it in her head.

"How was your relationship with your parents?" Marlene asked, her tone light but to the point.

"Well, Doc," Laura started, giving her friend a little grin.

"Hey, I may be your friend and all—but I've got skills you know," Marlene cut in, grinning back. "Go on."

Laura ran the palm of her hand around the back of her neck. "My father," she began again, "he was a strict man, but I believe he loved me very much." She paused. "He died before I got married, and obviously he never got to see Gwen either." She frowned then. "My mother was a cruel woman... I think she resented how much my father loved me. My father and I both liked to read, and I don't think she liked that I focused on my studies so much... because she'd said once, *'Being a housewife was good enough for her, why should I strive for more?'* She had even said to my father that I wasn't that smart and shouldn't get my hopes up about going to college... but I had good grades. I think... I think she was jealous... I would never raise my daughter in such a way." Laura took in a sharp breath.

"That's horrible, Laura. And you have done a wonderful job with Gwen—you should be very proud," Marlene said, her voice lifting at the end.

"I am... I'm over-the-moon-proud, I have to say," Laura said, a lightness filling her. She had been a good mother to Gwen, though it hadn't been easy. That was the understatement of the last 20 years, but they had both made it, survived the endless moving and instability. All she needed to do was make sure to keep herself steady, keep her eyes, ears, and senses attuned to what might be coming her way. In the meantime, she was going to do her best to live her life. There had been no new postcard directing her to stay or go, and maybe there never would be. She had to learn how to stop worrying about what *might* happen and focus on what she could control.

"And Gwen is graduating in a week—how great is that?" Marlene said, adding to the levity that was growing inside Laura.

"Thank you for listening—for understanding," Laura said.

"Hey—it's what I do, and I actually make a living at it," Marlene said, huffing a breath on the fingernails of her right hand, then she rubbed them against her blouse. "Say, how about we take another crack at going out—just for drinks, and people watching?"

Laura took in another sharp breath and held it. "Okay," she said on the exhale. "I can do this."

They had agreed to try the same restaurant, but this time Laura had opted for dress pants and a blouse instead of a dress. She was much more comfortable in pants and this second outing was all about creating comfort. Her outfit wasn't anything fancy of course, and it had been the outfit she'd used for her interview with the bakery. She had gotten the job, so it couldn't have been that bad, and the top and pants still fit her. She wasn't going out to impress anyone, she just wanted to spend time with her friend and enjoy her company while *'people-watching'*, as Marlene had said. She didn't bother switching her purse this time, as the satchel with the strap felt much safer and comfier than the small clutch had.

When Laura arrived at the bar, it was packed, and she couldn't see Marlene anywhere. Apparently, they were having a *Two-Drink Tuesday* for, well—no reason at all, it seemed, Laura was told when she had asked the hostess at the door. Then, over the tops of some of the patrons' heads, she spotted Marlene's own popping up above the crowd. She had obviously noticed Laura and was now waving both arms over her head, signaling for Laura to come to where she was.

Laura smoothed back her hair, then made her way through the tight crowd of what appeared to be mostly businessmen and some business women based on their office attire, though some men were wearing business casual with just dress pants and button-down shirts. Laura's outfit fit in fine as she had on navy dress pants and a white blouse, and similar in style to what the women were wearing, minus a matching blazer.

"Laura!" she heard Marlene bellow over the now loud music in the bar area as she pushed passed the last of the people between them.

"Hey—wow, busy," Laura said, raising her voice to be heard. "No table?" Marlene had been standing off to the side they had previously sat at, but she wasn't at a table this time.

"These guys are just paying their bill," she told Laura, pointing to the three businessmen next to her who were standing at rather than sitting at the small table that was in the middle of them.

"It's all yours, ladies," one of them said, as they passed by to advance through the crowd.

Marlene quickly slid into one of the bar-top chairs. "Hurry — grab a chair before someone takes it out from under you." Laura shifted into the chair closest to Marlene, leaving the empty one of the three out in the open. "I already ordered us drinks," Marlene said, turning in her chair toward the service bar.

Laura, not knowing what to do with herself, joined Marlene in staring through the packs of people towards the bar. Along the main bar area, she noticed there were mainly middle-aged men, lined up elbow to elbow, leaning on the bar, either facing towards or facing directly away, as if the spot they occupied was prime real-estate. Maybe it was, she thought, since any women needing to order a drink, other than flagging down a waitress, had to get past their line of defense to even be heard by one of the bartenders. That meant each woman trying to get a drink had to ask them to move aside or squeeze in next to them. Either way the men would get the opportunity to make small talk with them, maybe buy them a drink, or if they were desperate, they could *accidentally* rub up against the woman trying to squeeze in.

The waitress arrived then with four blue drinks on her tray. Laura didn't know what the drinks were, but she was thrilled she would not have to manage her own way to one of the bartenders.

"Blueberry Cosmo," Marlene said.

Laura watched as the waitress slid two of them her way. "Two-Drink Tuesday — enjoy," the waitress said with a smile, "Oh — and don't forget to fill out a trivia question ballot for the trip — drop them off in the box at the main door," she said before turning and moving sideways through the throngs.

"Check these out," Marlene said, lifting one of the coasters on the table. "Name five popular movies filmed in Hawaii. Oh — I've got this one." Marlene took a pen from her purse, then she began saying and filling out her answer in the space under the trivia question. Laura watched as she wrote,

50 First Dates

Jurassic Park & Jurassic World
Raiders of the Lost Ark
From Here to Eternity
Blue Hawaii

"Jurassic Park, I saw that with my daughter," Laura said, but was still unfamiliar with the others. She picked up a coaster and read, "How many islands are there in the Hawaiian Islands?" She looked at Marlene who shrugged. "I actually know this one," Laura said, with a grin. She had liked geography in high school. Marlene handed her the pen and then Laura wrote and spoke her answer out loud. "There are 8 main islands, but there are 137 in total."

"Here—give me yours," Marlene said, filling in both email address contact parts with her own. She knew Laura didn't use email. Then she got up from her chair. "Watch my seat—I'm going to drop these off—I'll be right back." Then she was gone in the direction of the hostess stand, swallowed by the crowd.

Laura guarded Marlene's open seat while watching the people around their table as though someone might literally take them out from under her.

"Done!" Marlene announced, slipping from the pack and into her seat again. "Cheers!" she said then, lifting the first of her two blue drinks. "Who knows—we might win, it *is* a trip for two."

Laura had travelled a lot, just not outside of the United States. She lifted the fancy glass then and clinked it against Marlene's. "Cheers!" she said, and then they both took a sip.

The drink tasted like summer, Laura thought, the sweet blueberries of late August. She and Gwen had gone blueberry picking several years ago here in Ann Arbor. It had been one of those *you-pick-it* farms they opened to the public near the end of August. "Mmmm," she said, "This one tastes better than the red one."

"Ya, the red one was cranberry, and it can be a bit tart—depending on how it's made," Marlene informed her. "How are you feeling?" Marlene twisted right and left in her chair as if indicating the question was about how she was doing with all the people around her.

"So far so good," she said, but was slowly realizing they weren't going to be able to have much of a chat with all these people around and with all the commotion. She had no intention of shouting her personal issues over the noise, so people watching and small talk it would have to be for now. "How was the rest of your day?"

Marlene laughed, as if grasping Laura was trying to make the best of their *loud* situation. "I didn't do much after seeing you at the bakery, just went home, returned some calls, then ate some leftover pasta I'd had in the fridge." Marlene tipped her drink back. "You?"

"The usual, make magic from dough," she said, then took another sip of her drink, a much larger sip than the first, then she grinned at Marlene.

"It really is magic—isn't it?" Marlene squinted, suspicion crossing her face.

Laura laughed, as she made a gesture with her hands over her drink, mimicking that of a magician. Then she picked up the drink and downed it. "Presto—my drink is gone," Laura added, following up with another laugh.

Several hours and several more drinks later, Marlene was teaching Laura the words to the anthem—Marlene had called, 'We Will Rock You', by Queen, as it blared through the bar. All the songs from the band had had a resurgence ever since the 'Bohemian Rhapsody' movie had come out, Marlene had informed Laura. Laura didn't know the movie, hadn't known who *Queen* was, but she was happy to learn and sing along. She was most definitely drunk. But she *was* having fun, and the more she drank the less she thought about how scared she was, and the less she cared that they were surrounded by strange men. That was until one of them decided he would take the open seat at their table, not take it away, but sit down in it at their table.

"Professsssor Weeeick," Laura slurred out, then tipped back the last of her latest blue drink.

"Christiaaan," Marlene said, slapping her colleague on the arm. "Welcome-welcome—can I get you a drink?"

"Thank you—no, I'm good," he said in response, lifting the bottle of his still cold and frosty almost full beer. "Are you guys having fun? I saw you ladies belting out the words to the last song."

"Aaanthem," Laura said, correcting him like she knew better.

"Right—it's a classic," he said. "I take it you like Queen, yes?"

Marlene waved over to the passing waitress. "Two more please," Marlene said.

"None for me," Laura said, horribly aware that she was now seeing two waitresses when she should only see one. She turned back to the professor. "Never heard of themmm," she said, in answer to his question.

"You've never heard of Queen?" he said, mockingly. "How could you not know Queen, have you been in a cave for the past thirty years?" He moved his chair closer to Laura.

Laura nodded. "Bassssically yaaa," she said, her head bobbing still as she leaned her elbows on the table.

The professor picked up one of the coasters. "What sport was invented in Hawaii?" he asked, reading the question off the back of it.

"Suuurfiiing," Laura responded.

The waitress returned then, quickly sliding the drinks across the small table to Marlene, causing Laura to sway. She turned her head back toward the professor as he took a pull on his beer, then set the bottle on the table next to her. The smell of the beer nearly made her gag.

"Are you okay?" Marlene asked her.

"Just feeeeling a little lightheaded, Laura said, leaning on one elbow.

"Did you eat?" the professor asked, a hint of judgement edging his voice.

"I didn't have time to eat, I had to finish orders before leeeaving work—had to russsh to get here," Laura said. She definitely wasn't feeling well, and she was now starting to feel hot, too hot in fact, and this guy was leaning in so close she could feel the warmth radiating from his body. "I should go," she said.

"Maybe we should both go," Marlene said, shifting to get off her chair. "I think I've had my fill too."

Marlene's words were a relief to Laura's ears. Fresh air, that was what she needed, and to get away from this furnace of a man. "Excuusss me," Laura said, moving off her chair to shove past him.

"Let me walk you ladies out," he said, getting up from his chair too.

"Thank you, Christian. That's kind of you," Marlene said, linking her arm now with Laura's. "Let's go Baker-girl."

Marlene guided the two of them out past the patrons and through the main door, but when they hit the fresh air, Laura wobbled. If it hadn't been so crowded, Laura thought she might have been able to make it out herself, but she was grateful to have Marlene to lean on now.

Further back along the street near the restaurant's parking area, there were several taxis lined up, and Marlene waved her arm to signal one over. "Have you got cash for a taxi," she asked Laura.

That's all she had, Laura thought. She didn't have a credit card, only a debit card, and she'd only gotten that when she'd needed a bank account to get Gwen and herself the cell phones. "Yup," she said to her friend. When the taxi pulled up, Christian opened the car door for her. "Thanks, Professssor," she said, sliding into the back seat. When he closed the door, Laura rolled down the window to hang her arms out. "Marlene," she called to her friend, arms spread out for a hug. Marlene leaned down and gave her a hug and then kissed the side of her head.

"Were to?" the driver asked.

Letting go of Marlene, Laura slurred out her address. "Byyye," she said, waving to Marlene. As the cabbie drove off, she was still waving, but when he took the corner at the end of the block, she was flung back into her seat. She slouched then and closed her eyes, leaning her head back against the seat.

Laura woke with a startle as the taxi came to an abrupt stop. "That'll be blaablaablaa," she barely heard the driver say as she lifted her head. She padded the seat beside her in search of her purse. Seizing it, she stuck her hand in under the flap and pulled out her wallet. Then she drew a twenty from the fold and handed it to the guy. It had cost her seventeen dollars to get here so a twenty would be plenty she figured. "Keep the change," she said, struggling out of her seatbelt to open the door. She had barely gotten out of the car and shut the door before the taxi had sped off down the road.

Standing now at the edge of the walkway into her housing community, Laura wondered how late it was. She had no idea, though she was aware of how dark and quiet it was, oh, and how drunk she felt. She turned then in a slow careful circle surveying the street.

There was nothing but the glare of the dim streetlights off the wet road that she could make out in the darkness beyond were she stood. It must have rained earlier when she'd been in the restaurant. She flung the strap of her purse over her shoulder as she turned back towards the path to her housing community, and the motion caused her to sway and stumble a bit. She noticed then that the small lights that normally lit the pathway, were not on for some reason, so she was going to have to take this slow and steady if she was going to make it to her house without falling and cracking her head open.

Before taking a step, she reached into her bag and pulled out the small flashlight she always kept for emergencies. The power had gone out at the bakery once and it had come in handy then. She switched it to on, and the path ahead of her shone to life. Then she took a step onto the curb but missed, scraping the front of her shoe on the edge. "Okay, Laura—get it together," she whispered to herself, making another attempt to step up.

She had only taken a few steps forward when a crash sounded to the left. Laura turned to shine the light in that direction, but the sudden movement caused her to trip again as she stepped off the path and onto the wet grass. Her foot slipped out from under her and she slammed down hard onto the ground. Not only was she drunk, now she was wet *and* drunk, and was going to have a nasty bruise on her hip from the fall. Aaand the lit flashlight she had been holding was now off and lost out into the wet darkness. "Dammit," she said, not as a whisper, and rolled to her opposite side to push up onto her knees. There was no getting around it, she was soaked now, so who cared if her knees got wet too. Steadying herself she got to her feet.

She knew the general direction of her home, so with her hands outstretched, she shuffled her feet along the grass until she hit the paved path. Lifting a foot, she cautiously stepped onto the path, then turned slowly in the direction she knew was towards home. One step at a time, she moved, slow and sort of steady, she made her way to the area softly lit by the front door lights of the houses.

At the end of her walkway to her house, she took the three steps up to the door. Another crashing sound rumbled behind her and she turned. She stared out into the darkness, the overhead door light marring her night vision now. Footsteps echoed, slow and heavy on the approach and heading her way. She turned back to the door with a wobble, rifling through her purse to find her keys. Finding them, she fiddled to get the right one in the keyhole. When the key turned, she twisted the doorknob and pushed open the door, then promptly stepped inside, slamming the door shut to lean against it. She was breathing so hard she thought she might throw up, and she slid to the floor too drunk and too unnerved to do anything else. It was then that she realized the entry light in the front hall was also out. She had purposely left it on knowing she might be late.

The sound of her heart pounded in her ears causing her to feel even more ill. She tried to take in a cleansing breath but doing so only made her feel more nauseous. Again, she squinted into the darkness now of her home, willing her night vision to identify the objects normally within view of the front door. She could almost make out the entry table and the edge of the opening into the main area of the first floor.

Laura squinted again, just as someone banged on the front door, and she nearly peed her pants. "Laura? It's Mrs. Gregson— your neighbor. Is everything alright?" The woman banged again. "My husband said he thought he saw you, saw you fall."

Laura leaned forward and pushed to her feet. "Hi Mrs. Gregson—I'm okay. I fell, yes—but I'm fine. Thank you for checking on me," Laura called through the door to the woman on the other side. Then she turned and kicked off her wet shoes.

"The lights are all out on the grounds—my husband called the 24-hour service line, but they can't come out until tomorrow," her neighbor informed her.

"Tell your husband—thank you, as well. Good night," Laura called, as she slid her shoulder along the wall towards the opening to the main area of her home. Through the opening, she found her way across the first floor to the bottom of the stairs with the help of the dim front-door light stealing through the mostly closed curtain in the living room. From the bottom of the stairs, she could see that the light in her bedroom was on, its glow peeking out from a crack in the door. It gave off enough illumination for her to get her bearings, climb the stairs and find her way to her bedroom.

In her room, she stumbled through peeling off her wet clothes on the way to her tiny en-suite bathroom, which was simply a toilet and sink, she'd had to share the shower in the other upstairs bathroom with her daughter. Laura switched on the bathroom light, then leaned against the sink to stare into the mirror.

She was a mess. And she was disappointed with herself for drinking so much, but she was more frustrated with herself for letting her guard down. She stuck out her tongue, then groaned.

It was *blue*.

Chapter 11

Scott pulled the ambulance up to the gate and then leaned out the window to speak to the man in the booth. The area was one of those neighborhoods that had the security guard out front and you had to get permission to get in, and it was at a location with very low call volume, so if you got a call, it was usually pretty serious.

They had been at the end of their shift when they'd gotten the call from dispatch, instructing that they needed to go priority 4, lights and sirens, on a *shots fired, possible suicide,* to this affluent neighborhood in Berkeley. The neighbor's nanny had called 911 after the 10-year-old boy she took care of, had said the guy who lives next door was parked in his driveway and that the boy thought he had heard a gunshot earlier when he'd first woken up. They had been given no other information, other than the boy had locked himself in the house, and police were already en route as it was *their* dispatch that had gotten the call first.

The guard waved them through the security gate, just as their own dispatch informed them the police had arrived on scene, that they had secured the scene, and there was an adult male in his car with a shotgun wound to his chest.

They pulled up to a house that had a three-car garage and was just as huge as the rest they had seen on the lengthy drive in, this one was not on, but near to the golf course that catered to its wealthy residents.

Gwen got out of the ambulance and walked over to a late-model BMW. It was her turn to run the call, and she noted that none of the doors or windows of the car were open. It was not running and there were no lights on, nor was the radio playing. On-site, there were four police officers, one in particular was hovering around the car, and he looked like a veteran cop, Gwen noted, as he didn't seem fazed by this scene at all. Then as Gwen reached for the door handle, the officer said, "Oh, he's obviously dead—you don't need to mess with my crime scene."

Gwen pulled back and looked through the driver's side window to see a male in his mid-50s, lifeless in the driver's seat, a shotgun propped between the steering wheel and the guy's chest. His hands were sitting on his lap, palms up, as if he were meditating. His eyes were wide open, head resting on the headrest, and his mouth was slightly open with no blood showing. He was not breathing and not moving. Gwen could see he was dressed in a denim shirt, two buttons done up at the top but the rest of the shirt was open, and he had a white t-shirt on under it, the hem of it pulled out over his jeans, but she couldn't be sure about his feet. And other than a clear bloody blast injury where the gun was still propped on his chest, she couldn't see any significant signs to tell her that he didn't have a pulse. She knew he didn't qualify for *obviously* dead just by looking at him, she had to put her hands on him. "I have to go in the car," Gwen said, noting that the officer was getting a bit feisty and seemed upset now that she was going to mess with his forensic evidence.

"Don't touch anything. Don't you know a dead man when you see one?" the officer said, resting his hands on the sides of his utility belt.

Being her supervisor, Scott stepped in then, and said, "Clearly you have no respect for her medical authority." Scott turned to look at Gwen, then back at the officer. "She has to," Scott stated, emphasis on the *has*.

With that, the officer shut up, but he didn't leave his position at the passenger side window.

Gwen opened the door; it was particularly warm in contrast to the cooler morning air. It smelled like motor oil, cigarette smoke, and gun powder. "Had the car been running when they got here?" she asked the officer.

"No," he said, "and no one other than you has touched any of my crime scene."

"There is no obvious significant blood loss and no pulse," Gwen stated. Now she had to draw back the two shirts away from the neck area to look at the wound without disturbing the area of the gun shot. Gwen saw then that the blast had blown the man's intestines out of his body, but they had been so neatly tucked inside his shirt that it had not been evident initially. Now he fit the *obviously dead* criteria and she didn't need to touch him anymore.

As Gwen was leaning back out of the car, another police officer was escorting the 10-year-old boy from next door, out of the house, right by the open door to the car. The kid, small for his age, had on his school backpack and had clearly been crying, and now he had a full view of the origin of that gunshot he had heard. They were on a three-car-wide driveway and the female police officer had to go and walk him right by the car. Gwen shook her head and then glanced back at the man in the car.

She leaned in to see two small marks that looked like taser burns on the side of the guy's jaw, and there was a two-inch wide band discolouring the skin of his neck. When Gwen leaned out again, Detective Franklin was pulling up alongside the BMW in a dark blue Crown Victoria. He got out and circled around to the side of the car Gwen was standing at.

"Brad Stinson," Detective Franklin said, leaning down to look into the car. "He worked with my dad back in my hometown."

"There's something you should see, Gwen said. "Check his neck."

"Neck? I thought this was a shotgun wound to the chest."

"It was—is, but something is off. Looks like he was tasered in the head and then strangled, *then* shot. The bruising is showing around the neck—same as the others."

"Others?" he asked, straightening. Then he barked out an order to the officer who had been doing all the hovering. "Get your forensic guy over here. We need photos of his head and neck—all sides." The officer just stared at him. "Now!" Detective Franklin shouted. "Good catch," he said, turning to Gwen.

Once the photos and details were taken, Detective Franklin suggested Scott and Gwen meet with him again at the diner. And like last time, they swapped out their rig for Scott's truck to drive over to meet up with his dad.

"Coffees—all around, please," Detective Franklin said to the waitress. When she left, he said, "Stinson was younger than my father, but he has been on the force a long time. He moved here nearly 20 years ago with his wife, she's a lawyer. He's a captain now—or was."

The waitress dropped off their coffees, and said, "I'll be right back to take your orders." Then she was off again.

"Before we left the scene, we found out he was going through a divorce and the wife had kicked him out of the house. He shouldn't have been there," Scott said. "The nanny next door said he had been in the driveway the other day, shouting at the wife, threatening to hurt himself."

"Yes, I know—I got a similar rundown on the way there," Detective Franklin said, before taking a sip of his scalding black coffee.

Gwen winced, then said, "That's pretty cruel—if his intention was to kill himself in the driveway so his wife would find him and be traumatized forever. But it was that little boy—the neighbor's kid, who would suffer all that trauma after seeing the body in the car.".

"I didn't know about the boy," Detective Franklin said. "And you're right, Scott, he shouldn't have been there, but what makes this case so intriguing, is that we need to determine if this was a murder or a suicide or somehow both."

"The marks show the same MO as the serial killer, but this time it was a cop instead of a professor," Gwen said, adding more to the detective's bemusement.

"Not like a serial killer to change MOs," he said, "but the killer had been dormant for six years, prior to that professor being killed at your college." He sipped his coffee again. "I'm not sure why the killer would murder him, but he was an ass, from what I remember," he said, shaking his head.

The waitress came back then to take their orders.

Once the food was on the table, Detective Franklin went on to tell them about several old serial killer cases in Michigan. "*Donald Murphy, Vitor Malone, Benjamin Atkins,* and *Shelly Brooks,* most of their victims were involved in the sex trade. And some of these killers never got convicted for all the murders they had actually committed. Like with *Coral Eugene Watts,* dubbed the 'Sunday Morning Slasher', he was convicted in the deaths of two Michigan women out of the dozens he was believed to have killed between 1974 and 1982. He got immunity for a dozen murders as part of a plea deal and was almost released on a technicality in 2006. He died of prostate cancer in prison."

"He deserved worse," Gwen said, stabbing at her scrambled eggs.

Detective Franklin nodded.

"Wasn't there some guy who was arrested for kidnapping and attempted rape in a Springfield Township cemetery?" Scott asked.

"Correct," his dad said. "*Leslie Allen Williams*, a parolee. The police discovered the victim in the trunk of his car. He then confessed to the abduction, rape and slayings of four teenage girls in rural Oakland and Genesee counties back in 1992."

"Wow—he confessed to others," Gwen said, glancing at Scott.

"Sometimes they get someone on a lesser charge to eventually get them for more later, because they don't have the evidence to arrest them for the worse crime. Right, dad?" Scott asked.

"Right, like with *Don Miller*, he had tried to rape a 14-year-old girl in her bedroom, but he was arrested before he could strangle her. He was sentenced to 30 to 50 years in prison for rape and attempted murder. Then months before he was sentenced, he was indicted on murder charges in the deaths of two women, one of whom had been his fiancée. He also admitted to killing two other women." Detective Franklin paused then to wave over at the waitress, then he lifted his coffee cup as to request more. He turned back to them, and said, "Then there's *Anthony Guy Walker*, who was already in prison for a rape conviction, was later charged in the cold case murders of three women. Then as part of the plea deal in the case, he admitted to two other murders, one he arranged to have killed in prison."

"Did you ever hear about 'The Michigan Murders'?" Scott asked Gwen.

She shook her head.

"I wouldn't have thought so," Detective Franklin said. "It was back between 1967 and 1969, way before your time—and mine, but they were a series of publicized killings of young women in the Ann Arbor/Ypsilanti area of Southeastern Michigan." The detective stopped when the waitress came to the table to fill his coffee cup.

"The guy was known as the *Ypsilanti Ripper*, the *Michigan Murderer*, aaaand the *Co-Ed Killer*," Scott said, when the waitress left, adding to the story.

"The victims were young women between the ages of 13 and 21. Are you sure you want to hear this?" Detective Franklin asked her.

Gwen nodded. "Go ahead," she said.

"Okay, well, these women were abducted, raped, beaten and murdered, typically by stabbing or strangulation, and then... their bodies were often mutilated after death before being discarded within a 15-mile radius of Washtenaw County."

"Holy crap—who was this guy?" Gwen asked, pushing the plate of her mostly eaten breakfast away.

"His name was *John Norman Chapman*—known then as *John Norman Collins*. He was arrested one week after the final murder and sentenced to life imprisonment."

"Well-good, I'm glad they got him," Gwen said, leaning back and crossing her arms over her chest.

"He was another one, he was never charged for the remaining five murders or the murder of a sixth girl killed in California, whose death had been linked to the series. The investigators believed he was responsible for all the murders," he added.

"He was only 21," Scott said, making a sour face and a scowl.

"Average age for a male serial killer is 27," Detective Franklin said.

"I'm just glad they caught him," Gwen said. "But how are you going to get this guy who's back—killing here, in your county?"

Detective Franklin gave his head a few slow shakes back and forth. "I guess I'm just going to have to go back to the beginning, go over the evidence again from the previous murders. There isn't much to go on, no DNA, nothing is ever left behind, and we only have a few images of the guy on camera, and only from the back and side. He wears work boots, a dark trench coat over similar coloured pants and shirt. He's always wearing a baseball cap and sunglasses, and he uses gloves—no fingerprints. Plus, you can see the black gloves in the photos and videos. He has dark hair and a beard, but we think the beard is fake, hair too possibly."

"Where were the locations of the last few murders, how close were they to here—the ones just before he disappeared, I mean?" Gwen asked.

"They weren't close," he said. "And I hate to admit it, but I have most—if not all the places and facts memorized, as I've been over the files so many times. But this last one... with Officer Stinson, it's really thrown me."

"Tell me about the others," Gwen said, unfolding her arms and leaning in.

"I'm going to need another refill," Detective Franklin said, tipping back the last of his coffee.

Gwen waved the waitress over.

Coffee cup filled now; Detective Franklin began the recap of the last four murder locations. "In 2010, it was at West Virginia University in Morgantown, West Virginia. The Professor had taught the master's program in accounting there. When he was killed, people were shocked but not heartbroken. The talk was that most had hoped he would have choked on his Werther's candy—he liked so much, a long time ago. Apparently, he had tenure at the university, and really did not teach, left it up to his teaching assistants to do the hard work while he took all the glory. He was a lech, and the female students had done their best to avoid him—he was well known for his bad behavior, but he was so old people were surprised he had any interest." He took a sip of his freshly poured coffee. "The professor was known also for saying things like, *'Most women are not good at math—these computers do all the work for them now, so they don't have to be good at it'*. There hadn't been much eagerness to investigate the death at first, but when I came in as a visiting detective from Detroit, I'd deemed it as part of the serial killings we'd been investigating." He grinned. "Slight change to the MO, as the guy was in his 80s, but the method was the same. Some thought because he was hated so much that it was just a copycat getting rid of the guy, and a few of the other accounting professors had been under suspicion, since they all wanted the old guy's spot on the faculty. But we got lucky, there was recorded footage of the man who did it, same guy as one of the other bits of video we had from an earlier murder."

"The key is in the details—I guess," Gwen said. "This death could have been missed as part of the series."

"Correct," Detective Franklin said. "Then in 2011, at Kenyon College in Gambier, Ohio, the Professor of Psychology was murdered, again same MO." He tapped the edge of his coffee cup with his spoon. "Then... in 2013, it was at DePauw University in Greencastle, Indiana, where the Professor of Film Studies was murdered. Ironically, there had been a video released before the murder, showing the professor and a young female student, revealing he had tied her up. He had tried to say it was *art*, but the student had said she'd been afraid he would fail her—or worse, hurt her, if she didn't go along. There had been a lot of he-said-she-said, but in the end, someone *had* taken him out." He nodded and then took another sip of coffee. "And the last one, before things went cold in 2013, was at Eastern Illinois University in Charleston, Illinois, the Professor of Exercise Science. I had been tracking the killer West across the states when he disappeared. Then, six years later, he shows up here, kills another professor, but *now,* he's changed his MO from professors to cops." He gave his head a firm shake as if frustrated and confused.

Gwen did the same, then took in an exasperated breath. "We lived in Charleston in 2013," she said then. There was something familiar about the name of that last university, in fact she was almost positive it was the same one that she and her mother had gone to for a nutrition class. "I was only fifteen then, but I bet my mother would remember hearing about that one on the news."

"How long did you live there?" Detective Franklin asked.

Gwen scrunched her face and shook her head. "Not long, just the summer. We moved to Ann Arbor that fall." She frowned, as an image of a man from that time scratched at the edge of her memory. Gwen's mother hadn't recalled knowing Detective Franklin, but her bet was that she might remember this police officer from her same hometown. And the last murder, the one before the case had gone cold, that subject was one more reason she needed to speak to her mother.

Chapter 12

When Laura had woken Wednesday morning, she had felt like death. This was what a hangover felt like, she had painfully realized. She had also realized that she was not going to make it into work, she could barely make it to the small bathroom off her bedroom to throw up. So, she had called in to say she was sick, and that had been no lie. She'd never called in sick in the six years she'd worked for the bakery, though she'd called in once or twice when Gwen had been the one sick, and the owners hadn't been upset when she'd told them this time that she wouldn't be coming in. She had returned a few texts to Marlene letting her know she was okay but had stayed home sick.

Laura had spent the rest of the day in bed, and she had only gone downstairs after dark to eventually get some food in her stomach. She had managed half a bowl of soup before needing to go lay down again, but she had made a point of double checking that she had left her keys on the side entry table. When she had stepped into the entry hall, she had not seen her keys on the table, instead she'd found them on the floor in front of the door. Off kilter then even more, she had moved towards the door only to find that it had not been locked, that the deadbolt had not been turned, and the security chain had been hanging unlatched.

Following a shiver down her back, she'd swiftly locked and fastened them all. She had let her guard down, gotten drunk and had left her front door open to the world.

Before she had returned to her bedroom, she'd padded around the first floor checking that the windows and the backdoor in the kitchen had all still been secured. And they were. When she had gone back upstairs, before going back to bed, she had taken a quick glance into Gwen's old room, for what she hadn't really known, and the room had been as it should have. Back in her bed, she should have felt better, safe, and been able to get some sleep, but she hadn't. She had had a restless night of crazy dreams and waking up squinting into the dark at shadows.

Now in the light of day, Laura pushed herself up out of bed, still angry at herself for being so stupid, for drinking so much, for having to miss work, and for not being clear-headed enough to lock up properly. She was also embarrassed, knowing she had more than likely made a fool of herself at the bar. Marlene had messaged her saying it had been a fun night, and that it had been entertaining to see Laura enjoying herself so much. She had been having fun, but when the drinks she'd had, settled in, she'd lost any decorum she had tried to maintain. Plus, she was mortified, because the night was a blur of faces, and dialog, and later panic as she had tried to get herself home. At least, she had made sure not to pass out still wearing the wet clothes and had managed to find her pajamas. Then she had spent the whole day and following night in them. Today she would text Marlene a more formal apology and let her know that she had paid the price for her lack of judgment.

In the kitchen Laura popped two pieces of fresh bakery cinnamon-raisin bread into the toaster. The sweet aroma of the slices toasting filled the kitchen and calmed Laura's nerves. She needed to get something more substantial into her stomach, and a few pieces of toast and butter she knew would do the trick. She picked her cell phone up off the table to check if she had any new messages. There were none. Then while her prescription for what ailed her continued to toast, she went to the front door to do another double check that the door was still secured.

Laura stopped short in the hall. There on the floor about a foot from the door, was one of those coasters, the trivia ones from the bar. She must have taken one, dropped it there the other night in her drunken stupor, was her first thought, but it hadn't been there last night when she'd locked up. Had she missed it somehow, she wondered then? She walked towards it as though it were something that might lash out at her. Then she bent slowly and picked the thing up.

It was definitely one from the bar, it had the same yellow and orange lettering and the hula girl on it as the others had that they'd filled out. She flipped it over, then nearly choked on the saliva she'd sucked in with her breath. On the flip side where the answer space should be blank, there was a message, and based on the handwriting and words, she knew it was from her stalker. The message read,

> *Did you have a good time last night, Laura?*
> *You looked like you were. Drinking and flirting.*
> *Enjoy it while you can but be careful.*
> *I am watching you, Laura, and I'm watching Gwen too.*

Two things Laura was now horribly aware of, her stalker was in Ann Arbor, and he had been at the restaurant the other night, maybe even that first night out with Marlene, and that he had been watching her. She had always imagined his observations of her were from a distance, but now she realized he had been in the bar, could have been standing near or even next to her, and she wouldn't have known it. She broke into a cold sweat and was once again feeling the need to throw up.

She made her way back to the kitchen still clutching the coaster and sat down at the table. She was not going to work today either, she just couldn't. She picked her phone up off the table and sent a quick text to her boss, stating that she was still under the weather and didn't want to put anyone at risk of getting sick, and that she'd be in tomorrow for sure. She sighed, setting the phone down, then the toaster popped startling her and she burst into tears.

She was so exhausted from this, from the fear, the taunts, and the confusion as to why this maniac had chosen to do this, chosen her as what, his devotional target, killing for her? But why and why her? She put her face in her hands and sobbed. Taking in a shaky breath she wiped a sleeve across her eyes, then looked again at the message on the table in front of her.

There was no mention of the murder of the professor, the one who had been killed at Gwen's school. There was no direction to stay or leave. And the stalker had not used a postcard from the previous town she had lived in either. This had been more up close and personal, using a familiar object from her night out, letting her know he had seen her drinking and enjoying herself. But she had not been flirting. The only man she had talked to had been Professor Weick, and it had hardly been flirting. If the stalker had been watching her that closely, it may have looked that way though. Could that be what he was referring to? Laura gasped in response when she saw the trivia question on the coaster. "What sport was invented in Hawaii?" she read aloud.

She dropped the coaster on the table, slid out of the chair, and then ran up the stairs, some two at a time, to the second floor. In her bedroom she went to her dresser and knelt on the floor to pull out the bottom drawer. Next to her other set of pajamas, she had a stack of manila envelopes. She slipped the one from the bottom of the pile marked *keep,* out from under the rest. Then she flipped the flap up and yanked out a stapled grouping of papers.

It was the article she had copied at the library all those years ago. She had read it several times back then, but she thought she had remembered something significant now that had been in it. She scanned the article. The doctor and his colleagues had identified five stalker subtypes, and in the article, they were defined as,

> The Rejected stalking type is an individual who has experienced the unwanted end of a close relationship, usually with a romantic partner, but it be could also with a parent, a coworker, or acquaintance. When this stalker's attempts for reconciliation fail, they commonly seek revenge.
>
> The Intimacy Seeker sees a person, often a complete stranger, as their true love and behave as if they are in a relationship with them. Many convey the delusion that their love is reciprocated. Celebrity stalkers tend to fall under this subtype.
>
> The Incompetent subtype, like the intimacy seeker, hopes their behavior will lead to a close relationship, fulfilling their need for contact and intimacy. But unlike the intimacy subtype, they acknowledge that their victim isn't reciprocating their affection but will still continue their pursuit. They are noted as being intellectually limited and socially awkward, and their inability to comprehend and follow socially normal and accepted dating rituals, they use methods that can be counterproductive and frightening.
>
> The Resentful stalker experiences feelings of injustice, and they desire revenge against their victim instead of a relationship. This behavior is about their perception that they have been humiliated and treated unfairly, and that they are the victim. They found that this type of stalker often views their fathers as highly controlling.

Laura had found it all very insightful, but the one she had been most interested in, the one that had sparked now in her memory, had been the last subtype, the 'Predator' stalker. This subtype was a person defined as *having no desire for a relationship with their victims, but they crave a sense of power and control, and that they find pleasure in gathering information about their victim, then fantasizing about assaulting them physically, but most commonly, sexually.* And like those motivated by a vengeful resentment, *there is often an acute sensitivity to the confusion, distress and fear resulting from their activities, and their difficulty establishing or maintaining intimate relationships lie at the root of many stalking episodes.* And it also stated that *many stalkers narrow their daily activities, focusing entirely on the victim and that collectively, stalkers have a remarkable ability to rationalize, minimize and excuse their behaviors, but that the most important step for managing stalkers is to see them as individuals in need of psychological help.* There was more, but it was more on how therapeutic interventions focused first on their mental disorders.

Ya, this guy needed help alright, she had thought even before reading the articles, and he was surely mentally disturbed, being both a stalker and a murderer. But the only references she had found in the article on murder *and* stalking together, had been those where the stalker was seeking attention from the person they stalked, or where they killed the person they were stalking. And there had been nothing in any of the other articles that referred to serial murders and stalking.

She had spent a considerable amount of time back then pondering why he might be following her, why he was killing for her, and how she might ever escape him. What had she done to incite this person to do such things? What could have motivated her stalker? Had she done something to this man that had warranted this behavior and focus on her? Laura had speculated about it all. Knowing that someone was watching you, following you, and well, *killing* for you, was not something the average person had to deal with.

A rapid knocking at the door downstairs ripped Laura's attention from her thoughts. Startled, she got up from the floor with the photocopy still in her hand. She left her bedroom and took the stairs slower this time and each step one at a time. The knocking on the door sounded again, louder this time and more rapid. "Who is it?" Laura called out from the first floor as she left the stairs.

"Laura?" she heard a familiar voice say, "It's Marlene!"

Laura dropped the papers on the dining table and then dashed to the door. She unlocked all the security and flung it open.

"Oh, thank goodness—I was beginning to worry," Marlene said.

"Come on in," Laura said, gesturing for her friend to come in. "Worried? Here, come sit at the table."

"My first appointment got cancelled so I have the morning free, and I was going to stop in to see you at the bakery—I called first, but they said you were home sick." Marlene pulled out a chair and sat down.

"I was going to message you this morning—I wanted to say sorry again for my behavior the other night," Laura said, sliding into the chair she had been seated at earlier.

"My gawd—I thought we'd had fun—no?"

"Yes, it's just..." Laura started to say, when Marlene cut in.

"There is nothing to apologize for," she said, as she crossed her legs. "Now, I've come to check on you. I am a doctor after all."

Laura felt herself flush.

"Or were you just playing hooky—I'm not intruding—am I?" Marlene uncrossed her legs.

"No—I'm not sick, and nooo you're not intruding either. Truthfully, I am grateful you are here," Laura said. "Can I make you some coffee?"

"That would be perfect," Marlene said. "

Laura got up from the table to get the coffee maker going.

"What's this?" Marlene asked.

Laura glanced back at her.

Marlene turned the stapled papers her way. "You're reading about the Mullen Study on stalking—what for?"

Laura flipped the switch on the coffee maker and then took in a long breath to summon up her courage. "I need to tell you something," she said. "I've wanted to tell you before—I guess I just wasn't ready. And I've never told anyone about this."

"What happened—what's going on?" Marlene asked, her expression shifting to one of intense concern, one Laura was sure her friend used often when dealing with patients.

"There's a reason that the guy staring at me at the bar upset me so much, it's not just that I'm terrible with men—I mean I am, but there's more to it." Laura then doled out the short version of events from the first town she'd lived in when Gwen was born and all the way up to the place they'd lived in before moving to Ann Arbor, explaining the stalking, the running, the postcards and now this latest stalking token, the coaster. She had left out the parts of the message that mentioned the murders, worried Marlene would judge her for not going to the police about the killings and the link she had to them. She had managed only enough courage to share this much and had felt relief at getting any of it out at all.

"Do you still have the postcards?" Marlene asked.

"No, I got rid of them, burned them—soon after I'd read each one." Laura pulled in a deep breath. "I didn't want them anywhere near us—needed them gone." Laura blew out the breath.

"Does your daughter know?" Marlene asked, leaning forward in her chair to put a hand on Laura's.

"No, but I plan to write Gwen a letter, outlining and explaining everything, why we had to move so much. I never told her before because I didn't want to scare her, plus I didn't know *how* to tell her."

Marlene patted Laura's hand. "We've talked about a lot of stuff, meeting for the past three years—sharing coffees and pastries. You're the reason I'm twenty pounds heavier than when we first met." Marlene gave a little laugh. "But please, know that when I say you can tell me anything—I mean it. I am sorry you felt you had to keep this from me. And I agree, Laura, it is time to tell your daughter. A letter is good, but make sure to give her time to digest it all though. She's going to have a lot of questions."

Chapter 13

Friday morning, early, Gwen was on the train out to Ann Arbor. The morning, despite being July, was exceptionally warm, and Gwen had chosen to wear cut-off jean shorts and one of her t-shirts with the paramedic logo on it, and she had put her shoulder-length hair in a ponytail. She had texted her mother saying she was coming for a visit, and her mother had responded with,

Two visits in one month. I must have won the lottery.

Her mother had also written that she needed to run an errand for the bakery this morning but would be back most likely by the time Gwen got to the house.

Gwen had wanted to get another look at those letters, and she wanted to talk to her mother about their time in Charleston. Plus, she was interested to know if her mother remembered the police officer from her hometown who had recently been murdered.

Gwen arrived to find the house empty, though she was met by the blissful air-conditioning and a delicious aroma of freshly baked cookies as she came through the front door. In the kitchen, she found a few dozen of her favorite cookies cooling on racks.

She grabbed one, then took several bites as she headed up the stairs to the second floor. She wasn't sure how much time she had, so she headed for her mother's room and straight to the back of the walk-in closet.

Her mother had never dated, that Gwen recalled, and with her father deceased, her hope was that they might be love letters from him to her mother. She had wanted to know more about her father, but like the topic of her grandparents, her mother had not liked discussing the past or her husband. She had told Gwen it was just too painful and that there really was not much to tell. They had been young; he was gone before she had even known she was pregnant and then all her focus had been on Gwen and taking care of their little family. The thin information had been enough for Gwen at the time, but it didn't mean she wasn't still curious.

Locating the letters, she picked up the stack only to find there were two black and white photos beneath them. The first appeared to be her mother, a clear younger version of the woman Gwen knew. The other was of her mother holding a baby wrapped in a floral print blanket, she guessed was her. Her mother had shown her a few other baby pictures of herself with the same blanket as this newborn baby was swaddled in.

"Gweeeen?" She heard her mother's voice call from downstairs, and no *Dolly* this time, she was grateful. She swiftly grabbed up the letters and shoved them and the two photos into her knapsack before leaving the bedroom closet. Descending the stairs and then setting her knapsack on the dining table, Gwen could hear her mother's voice and the familiar voice of Mrs. Gregson the neighbor, as they chatted at the front door.

"Hi Mrs. Gregson," Gwen said, rounding into the hallway. The older woman was in navy jogging shorts and a white oversized tank top and she wore a matching navy visor. She had great legs for a woman her age, as both she and her husband fancied themselves professional walkers as they were out each morning and evening walking the neighborhood. "How's Mr. Gregson?" Gwen's mom turned to grin at her. The old woman was sweet, a bit of a nosy neighbor but in a good way. She had a tendency to share the goings-on of the other neighbors, and Gwen's mother liked that someone else was keeping an eye on their little community.

"Hello, Dear. Oh, you know Mr. Gregson—he likes to keep a close eye on things around here. I was just checking on your mother to see how she was doing after her fall." She wiped the side of her face using a tissue, clearing away sweat from the now growing heat and her usual exercise.

"What—you fell?" Gwen said, moving in to get a closer look at her mother, checking for any visible bruises or cuts.

"Yes—I slipped the other night. The pathway lights were out, and it was wet, but I'm just fine." She widened her eyes at Gwen, then turned back to the neighbor. "Thank you, again Mrs. Gregson for checking on me—nice to know someone is keeping a watchful eye." She smiled at the neighbor.

"Alright then. Nice to see you Gwen," Mrs. Gregson said, with a wave as she turned and left the front step, then continued her walk up the path at a swift pace.

Gwen's mother closed the front door and locked it, then turned to face her.

"So, what's this about a fall?" Gwen asked again, this time with her hands on her hips.

Her mother shook her head as she moved passed Gwen towards the kitchen. "I'm fine, really," she said. "So, what brings you by to see your old mum for a second visit so soon?" Always the baker, Gwen's mom donned her apron over her faded knee-length denim shorts and white t-shirt, then began transferring cookies from the racks to a large plastic container. "You mentioned your friend Scott last visit, so I made an extra batch for you to take home."

Gwen grabbed another cookie off one of the cooling racks. "Thanks. He's going to die when he tastes them." She kissed her mother on the cheek. "Can't a daughter visit her mom?"

"Yeees," her mother said, placing the last of the cookies into the container before sealing it up.

"I thought I left my grey hoodie here, but I must have tossed it?" Gwen shrugged.

"That old ratty thing? I got rid of it after you moved out," she said, removing the apron and hanging it on the hook near the door to the laundry room. "You could have just asked me about it on the phone."

"Gwen nodded, then said," Well, I did have something else I wanted to ask you about."

"Everything okay?" her mother asked, crossing the kitchen to open the fridge. "Can I make you some breakfast — or are you full now from the cookies you've eaten?" She examined the contents of the fridge, shaking the container of almond milk as if to check what was left.

"Ya-ya, I just wanted to ask you about when we lived in Illinois — Charleston." Gwen slid her hands into the front pockets of her jean shorts.

"What about it? We weren't there long," her mother said, shutting the fridge door.

"How familiar are you with the 'Professor Murders'?" Gwen had not expected to go directly to the topic, but it had been weighing on her mind. "Do you remember hearing about the murder in Charleston — the one at Eastern Illinois University?" she added, being more direct.

Her mother leaned a hip against the counter. "Yes. I remember it."

"Was that when we lived there?" Gwen tightened her ponytail.

"Yes," her mother said, crossing her arms.

Gwen moved to lean a hip against the counter too, mirroring her mother. "Wasn't that the same university we did our nutrition course at?"

"Yes—what's this all about, Gwen?" her mother uncrossed her arms and straightened. Then she took one of the mugs off the dish rack next to the sink, turned the tap on, filled it with water and took a sip.

"Detective Franklin gave Scott and me the rundown on the case, told us about the last murder before things went cold —the one in Charleston. There's been another killing, but this time it was a cop—not a professor. And it's the same MO." Gwen crossed her arms then. "And you might know the guy."

Her mother lowered the mug nearly dropping it when she hit the edge of the counter with it. "You think... I might know the killer?" she gasped out, settling the mug next to the sink.

"Nooo, Mom, the guy who was killed," Gwen said, straightening then, letting out a chuckle.

As if flustered, her mother smoothed back her already-tidy pulled back hair. "How would I know this person who was murdered?"

"He was a cop from your hometown," Gwen said. "Bradly Stinson."

Without a reply, her mother picked up the mug again and moved across the kitchen to sit down at the dining table.

Gwen followed her to the table.

"I didn't know him," her mother said, "but from what I remember, people thought he was an ass." She took another sip from the mug.

"Ya—that's what I've heard too," Gwen said, followed by a laugh. "I should get going." She grabbed up her knapsack off the table.

"Your visits are so quick—can't you stay?" her mother asked, getting up from the table.

"I'll come back for another longer visit soon—I promise," Gwen said, going in for a hug.

"Don't forget your cookies this time," her mother said, hugging her a little tighter.

Unlike the arrival at her mother's place, Gwen's place was not empty when she arrived home. Having been given an emergency key, Scott had obviously used it to let himself in, because there he was, planted on *her* couch in mid-battle in some alien invasion game on *her* Xbox. "Welcome home," he said, as she locked the front door. "You gotta try this new game I just got."

"Tell me again, why it is that you always come here to play on my Xbox—when you have your own, aaaand you have the bigger apartment?" Gwen removed the container of cookies from her knapsack and set it on the small counter in the kitchen area of her studio apartment. Then she set her bag on the tiny counter-height island that took up most of the floor space in the kitchen.

"You've got the comfy couch and the bigger TV," he said, fingers clacking away on the buttons of the control. "You know that." He turned a quick glance her way, then turned back to the game in play.

The tan three-seater couch doubled as her bed at night. She had scored both the pull-out couch and the big TV from her mom's boss at the bakery. The boss and her husband had renovated and redone their living room after their two kids had gone off to college. The Xbox had been a splurge housewarming gift from her mother. Gwen figured it was her mother's hope she would be staying home playing video games versus going out in the evenings drinking, etc. And it *had* worked out that way, but she had never told her mom that. With working part-time and going to school, she'd not had time for much else than the occasional video game or meal at the diner. Even now, with all the shifts she'd been doing, the only person she really got to see was Scott. But she was cool with that, he was great company, and their friendship was important to her.

"Right," she said, pulling out one of the stools from under the tiny island. Like the couch, the island too had a dual purpose, functioning as a two-person dining table. "I have cookies," she added, before pulling the letters free from her bag.

The noise from the game came to an abrupt halt, and Scott was up off the couch and over to the kitchen before she even sat down.

"You've been telling me about these cookies for as long as I've known you—about time you shared the goods," Scott said, popping the lid on the container, grabbing up a cookie and taking a bite. "I can't believe you forgot them last time. Good thing you made a second visit."

"Mom made extra for you." Gwen sat down on the stool.

"Wandwan?" Scott asked through a mouthful of cookie. He chewed then swallowed. "Oh man—these are amazing. Think your mom would adopt me?" He shoved the rest of the cookie into his mouth, closing his eyes as if savoring what Gwen already knew to be heaven in a cookie.

"Didn't Detective Franklin already do that?" she asked, joking, and setting her knapsack on the floor next to her.

"Ya, but he can't bake," Scott said, grabbing up two more cookies before returning to the couch. "Make sure you tell your mom *thanks*—next time you talk to her."

"That will make her day—I'm sure," Gwen said, directing her attention back to the stack of letters.

They were bunched together by a thick rubber band that looked older than the letters. She gingerly removed the rotting tan coloured band and tossed it in the kitchen waste basket. The top envelope was faced down in the pile, and when she flipped it, she noted it had a faded post mark from April 1998, and was addressed to Muriel Rampton in Cambridge, Massachusetts. So much for love letters, Gwen mused. She moved through the stack to find they were all addressed to the same person, but the top letter was the only one that had been previously opened, the rest, thirteen in total, had surprisingly not been.

She removed and unfolded the one-page letter from the first envelope and found it addressed 'Dear Mother'. The handwriting appeared to be her mother's, and she figured the *Muriel* on the envelope to be her grandmother, but as Gwen read through the letter, her heart pained over the words that had been written, then she was hit unexpectedly with a wave of puzzlement as she reached the end and saw the signature. She believed she had been reading her mother's words, but the letter had *not* been from her mother, it had been signed, '*Love Rachel*'.

Gwen moved to the next letter in the pile, opening it to find the same, *Dear Mother* and signed *Love Rachel*. She opened the rest without reading them and verified they had all been addressed and signed the same. She swiftly read through the next three letters in the order. "Who the hell is Rachel?" she said, out loud.

"What?" she heard Scott ask from the couch. When she didn't answer, he prompted her again. "What are you reading?" He paused the game.

"Letters," she said, still scanning the fourth and fifth letters. "I found them in a trunk at my mother's place—thought they might be letters from my father to my mother, but no. Then I thought they were from my mother to my grandmother—looked like my mom's handwriting, but they're from someone named *Rachel*." Gwen only recognized the last name on the envelope and had made the assumption this *Muriel* was her grandmother, but now it was unclear who this person was.

"Does your mom have a sister?" Scott asked, coming over to the table.

"If she did—she never told me," Gwen said, examining the post marks from the first four letters.

Scott picked up the first of the letters, the one Gwen had set to the side of the pile on its own.

"That one is all about this Rachel person's father, her abusive father. Says he sexually abused her until she hit puberty, then he just beat her on a regular basis. It talks about her mother's indifference to it all too," Gwen said, tapping the edge of the letter Scott held with her finger. "It mentions how she went to the police to report the abuse, but they didn't believe her. Her father beat her after he found out what she had done. She felt her only option was to run away, the only way to be free of her father. The last part mentions how when she'd called her mother from the next town, that her mother had not cared where she was, and she had told her that after she'd run away—that the father had gone looking for her, had gotten in a car accident and died, *and* that the mother blamed her for his death," she added, glancing up at Scott.

"That's harsh—seriously messed up. But why would your mom have these letters?" Scott asked, setting the letter back on the island.

"No idea," Gwen said. "But here's the thing, the name on the envelope—the last name, it's the same as my mother's maiden name. But the kicker...." She picked up the stack of letters. "... these other ones, they don't talk about this Rachel's parents, they're all about her being stalked, and not just by some nut-job— no, she writes that he's a killer. How he always seems to find her in each town that she moves to. She's constantly moving, but he finds her. This one...." Gwen held up the second letter. "... it talks about her being in Hanover, New Hampshire and hearing about some professor of Art History being killed. This is where it all started—with the stalking. Each town she moves to, some professor at the local college or university, gets killed. These next four—after the one about the parents, they all reference the same towns your dad told us about. *Hanover, Brunswick, Middlebury,* and *Clinton.* This letter, the Clinton, New York one, ends with, *'If you've sent someone after me, you'll never find me'*."

Scott took the letter from her hand and scanned the page. "How many letters are there?"

"Thirteen," Gwen said. "I don't know if the date on the postmarks match, and there are no return addresses on the envelopes, but these first towns match the movements of the serial killer your dad's been tracking, Scott."

"Who the hell is Rachel?" Scott asked, picking up the next in the pile.

"That's what I said," she responded, sickened by what she had read, yet slightly excited at what she may have uncovered. "This guy isn't just stalking this Rachel person; he's killing people in each town she goes to, like a warning to her or something, maybe."

"But the serial killer disappeared six years ago," Scott said, as if pondering the facts.

"Ya—but he's back. Where the hell has he been all this time—and where is Rachel now?" Gwen slid the first letter back into its corresponding envelope.

"If this Rachel is still alive, she must be here—somewhere in Michigan," Scott said. "If not, why would he be here killing again—if he's doing it for her that is?" Scott reached over to grab another cookie from the open container on the counter.

"Look at these," Gwen said, pushing the next small stack of opened letters his way. "My mother and I lived in some of these same towns, and your dad mentioned these too, the last time we talked; *Asheville, Morgantown, Gambier,* and *Greencastle.*"

Scott pulled out the other stool from under the small island and sat. "Why didn't you say anything about it to him then?"

She shook her head. "The names rang a bell, but I wasn't sure of all the places—I was just a kid, but like I mentioned then at the diner, we lived in Charleston, Illinois—the place of the last murder before the case went cold. I asked my mother today if she had ever heard of the serial killer—and she said she had. She remembered that officer who was just killed too—from her hometown—didn't know him but knew his name." Gwen watched patiently as Scott scanned the next two letters.

"There isn't much in here," he said. "I mean, she says someone is following her—feels like she's being watched all the time. She mentions the professors being killed—but there're no details on the killer. She doesn't really state there's any proof that these killings are related to her, other than the corresponding cities, and she doesn't seem to know who he is." Scott pushed the letters back towards Gwen.

Gwen sighed. "Don't you ever get a gut feeling about something? These letters feel like something, Scott." She bent and pulled a pen and a small pad of paper from the inside pocket of her knapsack. Then she set the pad next to the stack of letters and began going through each one again, writing out the dates from the postmarks and the corresponding city mentioned in each of them.

"Hey—remember when we had to transport that psych patient from the police station to the mental facility? It was your first ride-along." Scott leaned the stool back far enough that he could rest his back against the kitchen counter.

"How could I forget *Crazy-Eyes,*" she said, blowing a breath through her lips.

"Ya the eyes don't lie. Mania can affect the entire eye, from changes in the distance between the brow and eye, changes in the lids, to pupils changing size *and* the iris changing color."

Gwen paused her writing and shook her shoulders as a shiver ran down her spine.

"They taught you how to recognize mania in the eyes, didn't they?" He brought the stool forward again.

"Ya—first year," Gwen said, tapping the end of the pen on her bottom lip. "If the person is in euphoric mania, you might see a shimmering quality to the wide-open eyes, but if they are in dysphoric mania, their eyes narrow and can appear to turn black." She shuddered again. "Crazy-Eyes was definitely in dysphoric mania."

"It's the adrenaline that makes the pupil take over the eye," Scott said, adding to the already freaked out feelings she was experiencing.

Needing a bit of comfort, Gwen reached over and took a cookie from the container. Then she nibbled the edge, contemplating her options. "Let me do some research on the dates and these other places," she said, switching gears. "Then I'll call your dad.

Chapter 14

After a little online research on the towns and universities and the corresponding postmark dates from the letters, Gwen felt there was no doubt in her mind that these letters from this Rachel, this information, all corresponded to the same serial killer Detective Franklin had been tracking all these years. She probably should have called him last night, but she wanted to be clearer of what she believed she had. Scott had given her his dad's cellphone number before he had left last night, and early first thing this morning she had texted him with,

> Hi, Detective Franklin. This is Gwen, Scott's friend. Do you have any time to meet this morning? I have something I need to talk to you about.

He had written back saying, for her call him. So, she did.

Setting her knapsack now next to the coffee table, Gwen sat down on her comfy couch, crossed her legs and leaned back, and then dialed his number.

He picked up after the first ring. "Hello—Gwen, funny you should message me—I have some questions for you," he said, but before Gwen could respond he asked. "Jamison, is your mother's married name, yes?"

"Yes," Gwen said, caught off guard by the directness.

"Sorry," he said, as if sensing her shock. "I've been going over the case files—I've followed up on all my leads and revisited all the people interviewed, and I came across a list of names of people interviewed in Lewisburg, Pennsylvania. And Gwen, it appears your mother's name was on it."

"My mother's name?" Gwen said, sitting forward on the couch.

"Do you remember living in that town?" he asked then.

"Uhm no—I don't know—what year was that?" Gwen shot a glance at the stack of letters now sitting on her coffee table. She had planned on going over them with him.

"2002—January," he said into her ear.

Doing the math, she said, "I would have been only turning four that year." She turned to look at the bouquet of construction paper flowers on the side table.

"Right... do you think there's a chance the two of you could have lived there at that time?" he asked.

They had lived in several of the other cities he had mentioned, she knew that already. Could they have lived there too? Could they have been in the same towns as Rachel, at the same time, at the same time as the killer? A tingling sensation ran across the back of Gwen's neck. These letters she had, they had something to do with this case, she knew it.

"You mentioned that you had lived in the same town as the last murder—before it went cold, I mean," he said, pulling her from her thoughts.

"Detective, how long would it take you to get to the diner? I think we need to meet," she said then, grabbing up the letters and shoving them into her knapsack she had set next table.

Gwen sat alone in one of the booths, during the early morning breakfast rush, twisting the wrapper from the straw that had come with her glass of ice water. It was another hot day, and

Gwen had worn her cut-off shorts paired with a white t-shirt, but she welcomed the cold air of the A/C at the tiny diner. Despite the chilly air, she was anxious and sweating, and the back of her thighs were sticking to the vinyl seat. Detective Franklin had confirmed on the call, that he could be there within the hour, and she turned then to look over her shoulder as the hour hit and just as he was entering in through the main door.

"Gwen," he said, sliding into the seat across from her. He always dressed very nice and was wearing navy dress pants and a short-sleeved dress shirt, though he was already sweating through it at the armpits. "I'm sorry if my questions upset you. I know it might be a stretch, but I had to ask." He gave a wave to the waitress when she looked over from across the diner.

Gwen shook her head. "That's the thing, I don't think it's a stretch." She balled the wrapper up and tossed it next to her empty glass. Not sure where to start, she said, "Rampton... my mother's maiden name was Rampton."

"Rampton—really?" he said, his words hinting at surprise and a touch of confusion. "I knew of a *Rachel* Rampton, but not a Laura."

"Rachel?" Gwen said, stunned, but then she should not have been surprised at these details leading back around.

"She was a girl from my hometown—her father was a professor at the college. She was a troubled girl—ran away, apparently." He rubbed his chin as if remembering something more. "Did your mother have any cousins?"

"It's possible—but she never talks about her family," Gwen said. Could Rachel and her mother be cousins? Was that why she had these letters?

"You asked me to meet you—is everything okay? Is Scott okay?" He dabbed at his sweaty forehead with one of the paper napkins.

"Yes, sorry—Scott is fine. It's not about him," she said, unsticking a thigh from the seat.

"Are you okay?" He leaned in.

"Ya—sorry," she said, trying to find the words to start again. "It's not about me—not really, it's about my mother. That's why I was so caught off guard when you asked about her."

"What about your mother?" he said, just as the waitress finally came by to fill his coffee cup. She placed another ice-water on the table in front of him.

"Uhm, well—I guess it's not really about her specifically, it's about these letters I found at her house." The detective frowned. "My mother had these letters—in a travel trunk. I've been through that trunk many times, but I'd never seen them before. I thought they were from her to her mother—my grandmother, but they weren't. I brought them with me," she added, patting the knapsack beside her.

"I'm sorry—but you've lost me here," he said, leaning back in his seat again. Then he picked up his coffee.

"They're from Rachel," she said, as if ripping off a band-aid. "To her mother."

The detective stopped mid-sip, the coffee cup inches from his mouth. "Why would these letters be of interest to me?" he said, before completing the sip.

"The first letter mentions Rachel's father," Gwen said. "The letters span years and mention her moving—a lot."

"The Rachel I knew disappeared," he said, frowning again, his eyes going to the glass of ice-water. Condensation was dripping down the side onto the table. He lifted it up and put a paper napkin under it. He looked back at Gwen, then took in a deep breath, and said, "I had gone out with the search party—trying to find her, her father went out searching too—not very hard, mind you. Guess he wanted to look like a concerned father." He rubbed a hand over his chin. "The guy may have been an English professor, but he'd been just a drunk that night. Practically drove me off the road. He died that night—crashed his car into a ditch. Rachel had gone to the cops the day before she disappeared, to report that he beat her." He glanced back over to the glass of water.

"I know," Gwen said. "It's all in the first letter." Gwen went on then to tell him about how the first letter talks about Rachel being sexually abused and that the numerous beatings came later after she had reached puberty, and how Rachel's mother had blamed her for the father's death. "But there's more," Gwen said. "The rest of the letters, they mention some man following her from city to city as she moved." Gwen then broke down the contents of the other letters, the places and the dates, the stalking *and* the killing, and the research she had done. She also explained that unfortunately, there wasn't really anything in the letters that could help him to identify this killer. And she had managed to get it all out and uninterrupted, she had noted.

The detective had appeared dumbfounded by what she had relayed to him, and he had barely looked up from staring at his coffee cup or that dripping water glass. "I don't understand why my mother had these, but they could be cousins—like you said," Gwen added, squirming a bit in her seat, unsure what else to say.

"I went out with the search party—like I said. But I've read the file." He glanced up at her then.

"Was there something more to Rachel's story?" Gwen asked, leaning forward to put her elbows on the table.

Detective Franklin took in a long slow breath, letting it out even slower. He turned to look out the large window, staring at nothing in particular, as people walked by, then said, "After she made her report to the police, they sent a cop to her home to investigate. The mother had given the police some story about her being a runabout and a liar, so the police didn't believe her statement." He paused and looked back to Gwen.

"What aren't you telling me? I'm guessing they never found her. Do you think the killer was after her then, was that maybe why she ran away?" Gwen asked. Her heart was pounding in her throat.

He looked away, then back at her again and visually swallowed. "That officer that went out to the house to investigate Rachel's claims... was the same officer who informed Rachel's mother that her husband was dead."

"And?" Gwen said, anxious to the tenth degree.

"That was Officer Stinson—the cop that we just found murdered."

Gwen's head was bursting now with all this information, yet she still had questions for her mother, as did Detective Franklin.

She gave him the letters to review, and he said it was imperative that her mother contact him as soon as possible, but he had also agreed to let Gwen speak with her mother first, and that was where she was headed now.

When Gwen got to her mother's house, she wasn't greeted this time by the scent of freshly baked cookies, and when she called out for her mother, all she heard in response was the sound of the A/C unit pumping out extra hard due to another hot scorcher of a day. She had wanted to speak to her mother, but she had also wanted to examine that trunk further, so she ran up the stairs to get another look.

Lifting the lid, Gwen found that the textbook, the one she had noticed last time labeled *Understanding the Classic American Novel*, was now wrapped in an old worn leather belt. She picked up the book and gasped. The author's name on the book read 'Professor Michael Rampton'. Detective Franklin had said that Rachel's father had been an English professor, this had to be him. The appearance of the old belt cinched around the book was unnerving and Gwen set the text back in the trunk. She pulled her phone from her knapsack's front pocket and checked the time.

She did not have a lot of time and needed to get back to town to get ready for her shift. Not wanting to wait any longer, she dialed her mother's cell phone. It went to voicemail. "I have the letters, Mom—and I want to know who Rachel is. Call me," Gwen said, frustrated, leaving her mother a message. She checked the time on her phone again.

Downstairs, she locked up, before heading back to the station, mumbling to herself about how she really needed to get a car.

She had made it back in time to change for work and had enough time in the ambulance bay now to get ready for her shift. She laced up her steel-toed boots, then straightened to readjust the pen in the pocket of her short-sleeved uniform shirt, then double checked the epaulet straps on her shoulders. They weren't permitted to wear shorts of any kind while at work, but it was going to be such a long hot day, she would have given just about anything to cut off the bottom half of these poly-cotton pants she was required to wear. She tightened her ponytail and came around the open backdoors of the rig then and saw Detective Franklin heading her way.

"Hey—it's good I caught you," he said as he got closer. "Scott mentioned you were on shift with him again today." He put his hands on his hips and glanced around the bay. "Were you able to speak to your mother?"

"No, she wasn't home—but I left her a message to call me," Gwen said, moving to shut the ambulance doors.

"Well—the letters match, Gwen. All the dates and cities." He looked around again as if checking to see who was in earshot of their conversation. "But there are some details in the letters that were not released to the public, so Rachel could potentially be a witness to some of these murders. If we could locate her, maybe she could help I.D. this murderer."

"Did you tell Scott about this?" Gwen asked, leaning around the rig to see if Scott was on his way back from filling up their water bottles.

"Not yet." He swiped at the sweat bead running down the side of his face. "I was wondering about the idea that your mother could be a relative of Rachel's, but I'm struggling as to why she would have the letters," he said.

"I wish I knew the answer to *why* as well," Gwen said. Obviously, her mother must have known Rachel, they had to be related. But what else has her mother been keeping from her all these years, Gwen speculated?

"They have to be related," Detective Franklin said, as if reading her mind. "Your mother must know her, and she may not realize that she knows who this man is — the one Rachel refers to in the letters, the one Rachel believes is the serial killer. Your mother might even be able to give me the first solid lead I've had in years. Maybe I could go see her — does she work in the city?" He wiped at the side of his face again.

"No, she works in Ann Arbor," Gwen said, exasperated. Then a sudden realization hit her. "We moved around a lot when I was a kid — I don't remember all the cities — but there were a lot. What if Rachel isn't the only one running from this guy? What if my mom was afraid of this man too — and why she's never come forward?" Gwen said. "I'll try her again." Gwen fished out her phone from the pocket of her cargo pants and then dialed her mother. "Voicemail," Gwen said, shoving the phone back in her side pocket.

"Hey, Dad," Scott said, rounding from the other side of the rig.

"Hey, Son," he said. "Sorry, but I gotta run. Gwen, you'll keep me in the loop, yes?" He gave his son a pat on the shoulder and then he turned to leave.

"Later, Dad," Scott said, handing Gwen a clipboard.

"Will do, Detective," Gwen tossed back, frowning then at his abrupt departure. "What's this?" She looked down at the paperwork clipped to the board.

"A work order. They have to run service on the rig before we can head out." He rolled his eyes. Then he opened the driver's side door, placed their water bottles in the drink holders, and then climbed in to sit and wait.

Gwen huffed out a breath. More delays, like she wasn't already frustrated enough with her mother not returning her calls, this was one more thing now to add to her growing annoyance.

An hour and a half later, when they were pulling up to attend to their first call from dispatch, Gwen's phone vibrated against her leg. Sliding it free from the side pocket, she saw it was her mother calling. She answered, and said, "I can't talk now, Mom— I'm on site."

"What letters?" her mother said back to her.

"You know what letters—the ones from Rachel. Who is she— a cousin?" Gwen undid her seatbelt and opened the passenger side door.

"I don't understand what you're talking about?"

"Look, Mom, you need to come in and speak to Detective Franklin, about those letters."

"Gwen, I don't want to talk to some detective—I need to talk to you."

"Mom, just call the County Criminal Investigations unit and ask for Detective Franklin." Gwen slammed the door shut.

"Let's go Gwen," Scott hollered from the back of the ambulance.

"Mom—I gotta go—just call him, please." Gwen hung up and slid her phone back into her pocket.

* * *

The overnight shift they had been on, normally ended shortly after 7 a.m., but they'd had to cover for part of the next shift, since unlike their rig, the other ambulance had needed to get extensive service done, not just reviewed as theirs had been.

Gwen was beyond drained now, so much so, that she had waited to check her phone until Scott and she had parted ways at their apartment floor, and she was out of her uniform and comfortably planted on her couch. That's when she saw that she had two messages waiting for her.

Checking the call log, she saw that one of them was from Detective Franklin, the other one was from her mother, and she pressed the voicemail button to listened to her mother's message first. She put the phone on speaker, then set it on the coffee table.

"Gwen, now I don't know who this Rachel person is you keep talking about and I don't have a clue what letters you're referring to," her mother's voice said, followed by a huff. "What I want to talk to you about involves your father." There was a sound of another huff. "We were never married. And, well—he's still alive."

"What?!" Gwen said, picking up the phone and staring at it.

"I didn't know him—not really... he, well—he raped me—it's the reason I changed my name. I'm sorry I didn't tell you before—but it's the reason we have moved so much—he's been following me ever since I left my hometown, and I don't know why."

"Mom—oh-my-god," Gwen said to her phone, stunned.

"Gwen—I don't know his name, but I think…I think he's this serial killer. He'd been gone for six years—I hoped he'd been arrested or dead even—but he's back, and he knows where I am."

The call ended then, and Gwen hit redial on her phone. "Voicemail again—dammit." *Beep* "Mom—Call me back," was all she said before hanging up and switching to hear the message from the detective.

"Hello, Gwen—it's Detective Franklin. Can you call me with an update?" was all his message said.

Gwen hit dial on the detective's number, but his voicemail too picked up. "Meet me at the diner right away—what I have to tell you can't wait," she said, leaving him a message. She had an update, and she had a theory too, now that her mother had given her this information about her father, but unlike her mother, it was not something she felt she could leave in a message.

Chapter 15

Last night was probably the worst sleep Laura had ever had. In fact, she felt like she had not slept a wink. She had been so distraught over her phone call with Gwen that she could barely calm herself enough to get any semblance of rest. And this morning she was a wreck, having not heard back from Gwen about what she had told her in that message about Gwen's father. She wouldn't be okay until she had a chance to speak to her, however she had got herself together enough to head into work for the early shift, mainly because she couldn't let herself miss another day of work again.

Laura had had two cups of coffee before leaving home, yet it was not helping with her lethargy. All it had done in fact, was frazzle her already fraying nerves. She was only past the first hour of work and she had already messed things up by charring two apple pies, by putting salt instead of sugar in the butter tarts, and she had backed up into one of the supply shelves when she'd clumsily burned her arm on a tray in the cooling racks. Now they would have to order additional supplies of vanilla, almond and peppermint extracts, as the boxes containing the bakery supplies of the extracts, had been on the shelf she had banged into, and they had all fallen off and smashed onto the floor. A couple of the bottles had been salvageable, but these few would not last awfully long in a bakery.

"*Accidents happen,*" her boss had said to her, but Laura had felt like an ambling disaster. This type of behavior her boss knew, was not typical, and sensing that Laura might not be herself today, her boss had sent her off to the local grocery store with the easy task of purchasing the extracts they would need. Laura knew that if she could just get the supplies they needed to get through today and tomorrow, they'd be fine until the new shipment arrived on Tuesday, and that she might be able to redeem herself over the screwups she'd made this morning.

Before going into the grocery store, Laura made a call to Marlene, but it went to her voicemail. "Hi, I need to talk to you — can we meet?" Laura said, when the message beep sounded. She could really use some wise words on how to handle things with Gwen. She slid her phone back into her bag as she entered the store through the sliding doors, then went straight to the aisle she knew the baking products should be.

In the middle of the aisle, the one she had been to dozens of times, she found that the section that normally displayed the shelves of flour and sugar and smaller baking supplies were nowhere to be seen. She looked to the overhead sign, and it clearly stated this was the baking aisle, however, instead of finding the urgent supplies she needed for the bakery to make amends, there were items such as loaf pans, muffin tins, cookie trays in several materials such as onetime use foil and reusable ones in glass, metal and that flexible silicone. The section was filled with tools for baking, and not the edible food items that were normally here and that she required. She turned left and then right to glance down the aisle, and at the end nearest the butcher section, she spotted one of the young male stock clerks. She waved to him for help, and he waved back, sauntering over at a less than amiable pace than Laura would have preferred.

"Good morning, ma'am. How can I assist you today?" the barely 16-year-old young man said.

"The other baking supplies—where have they been moved to?" She adjusted the strap of her bag on her shoulder.

"Other baking supplies, ma'am?" he said, as if she had asked for rocket fuel, then he turned to glance at the baking pans.

"Yes—the food items, like flour and sugar—they used to be right here," she said, motioning to the area with the baking tools.

"Right—yes, they were moved to a new section," he said, stating what she already knew as obvious.

"What section?" Her nerves were wearing thin with this kid.

"The section with all the spices and oils—same aisle as the pasta and sauces, and that sprinkle cheese stuff." He grinned as if the words he spoke were genius.

"What. Aisle. Would that be?" she asked, her patience waning.

"Next one over," he said, pointing in the direction of the next aisle.

"Thank you," Laura said, turning on her heels and heading down and out of the aisle to get to the next one. "The kid could have just said, '*next aisle*' first and saved me all the painful back and forth," she muttered to herself.

She rounded the corner to the aisle then only to find she had picked the wrong end of the previous aisle to exit from and was now at the side with all the pasta and sauces.

"Did you have a good time the other night, Laura?" came a man's voice from behind her, and she froze. "Laura?" the man's voice came again. The need to run overwhelmed her, but her feet remained bolted to the floor, and despite the adrenaline rush craving to propel her forward, she stayed where she was, struggling to muster whatever courage she could find. Drawing in a breath, she turned herself in a slow circle, her feet dragging as if pulled through wet cement.

The man standing before her, smiled. "I thought it was you," he said. "My apologies if I startled you."

Her nerves were still frazzled, yet she let her shoulders relax and then she blew out the breath she had been holding. Professor Christian Weick stood next to the short rows of pasta sauce, holding a green grocery basket, and grinning at her. "Professor," she said, feeling a flush of embarrassment now, remembering what her behavior that night must have looked like. "The other night, yes—it was fun. I don't normally drink that much—drink at all, really. Sorry if I was a bit out of it," she said, attempting to clarify and repair any damage to her dignity she may have sustained. She readjusted the shoulder strap of her bag.

"No-no, it was all in fun—I'm glad you enjoyed yourself. And call me *Christian*, please. Dr. Branden mentioned that the two of you don't get out much." He lifted the little green basket from his side to hold it in both hands.

"Yes," she said, the flush of humiliation returning.

"I'm just here to pick up some items for a dinner I'm preparing for a friend, though I'm not sure about the meal idea." He glanced at the shelves of pasta sauce. "I feel a bit helpless, really," he admitted.

"Helpless? With making pasta?" she asked, relishing the opportunity to make him feel a bit foolish. It was not nice, but she had already had a morning full of feeling stupid herself.

"I mean—I know how to cook the pasta and add the sauce, but when it's just for me, I don't worry about if it's good or not." He laughed. "But…" he started to say.

"But when it's for someone else—for a *date*, you want it to be… good, *special* even," Laura finished for him. She may not know anything about dating, but she did know about food.

"Yes, my thoughts exactly," he said. "Which of these would you choose?" He pointed to the shelves.

She came to stand near the sauces and tapped a finger on a colourfully labeled jar in the row second from the top. "These ones are the name brands and the most popular ones purchased. These...," she said, pointing to the top row. "these here, are made by smaller companies and taste more homemade. And those at the end there...." She pointed, then shuffled passed him. "These are the *organic* small company ones, and I would go with one of them, if I had to choose." He reached for the first jar, and she said, "That one has quite a lot of garlic, I would stick to the tomato and basil blend if this is for a date."

"Right—good call. I love garlic, though you're right about it not being great for a date," he said, grinning again, switching to pick up the version she had suggested.

She then moved up the aisle to the section with the boxes of pasta. "Go with spaghetti—it's the easiest to cook and the least likely to feel too filling." In contrast to the sauce she had recommended, she handed him a box of one of the popular brands available. "Best to go with a company who knows what they're doing on the pasta side. Homemade is best, but I take it this dinner might not be the ideal time to experiment with making pasta, yes?"

"Yes—simple and delicious is what I'm aiming for," he said, in agreement. Then he reached for a canister of cheese off the shelf next to the pasta. "Parmesan or Romano?" he asked, before picking and taking one from the shelf.

"Fresh," Laura said in response. "Come with me." She turned then and left the aisle the same way she had come in. She did not look to see if he was following her, she just assumed he was, if he genuinely wanted her help.

When she stopped in the deli area in front of one of the open cooler fridges, she turned to see him scanning the contents of the cooler next to the one she was standing at. "Never buy the processed stuff that looks like sawdust," Laura said, to get his attention. He stepped closer and leaned in to look at the display of cheeses. "Make sure it says *Parmigiano-Reggiano* and get the type that looks like flakes—similar to the fancy pastries you see with shredded chocolate."

"Brilliant," he said, full of enthusiasm now. "Should I get some of that garlic bread from the freezer section?"

She raised her eyebrows and gave him a smirk. She had not taken the time to consider his appearance that first meeting at the bench. Then, at the bar when he had come over, she'd been too drunk to scrutinize much of anything to do with his looks, so her recollection of him had been vague at best. Standing in front of her now she recognized that he was not bad looking, some might even consider him handsome.

"Right—no garlic. Does that cover it, do you think?" He placed a container of the shredded cheese into his basket.

"Not quite," she said, then checked her watch. "I still have to grab some things for the bakery."

"Don't let me keep you—you've been so kind to help me," he said, checking his own watch for the time.

"Do you know what kind of wine they like—your dinner guest?"

"Wine, no—I hadn't thought of that, and I don't know their preference." He gave her a little grimace.

Laura may not drink, but she had learned plenty about wine with her years in food service and running the catering. "Okay, so you get both, a red and a white. For white, since you are doing Italian food, pair it with a nice crisp *Pinot grigio*. For red, go with French, and pick a mid-priced *Cabernet Sauvignon*." She checked her watch again.

"Laura—thank you so much for your help," he said, rocking his carry basket of food. "And I'm sorry for keeping you from your own shopping."

"No worries, but I should get back to it." She gave him a kind smile. "Wines that way," she said, moving then to leave.

"Thank you, again," he said, turning in the direction she had indicated.

She started off in the way of the aisle they had come from, then stopped. "Oh, pick up something for dessert too—something light."

He turned back and nodded, then waved.

She waved back, pleased with herself for being brave enough to help him with his meal planning, and for even talking to the man. "Lucky lady," she said under her breath, smiling, surprising herself now that she had even considered the idea. Her smile dropped then when her reality slid back in, this time surprised that she had forgotten even for a moment why she was there. Then her thoughts turned to even more dreadful ones for what she would eventually have in store regarding speaking with her daughter.

Laura returned to the bakery, and luckily for her, she had found the supplies she had set out to retrieve from the grocery store. At least she had gotten that one of her tasks right.

She then spent the rest of the day working in the back helping to clean up, repair the damage she had caused, and remake any of the food she had ruined. Fortunately for her, it had been a slow day, and all she had left to do on her tasks was to move the remaining baked goods from out front in the display case into the refrigerated storage area in the back. And she was happy to do so, as it was just her now alone in the bakery.

She was heading to the back with the last of the large trays, when she heard the bell on the bakery door jingle. Funny, she thought she had locked the main door, but then she had gotten a lot of things wrong today.

"Hello," a man's voice call from the front area of the bakery.

A cold prickling crossed the back of Laura's neck making the tiny hairs at the nape rise. It's just nerves she told herself, and too much coffee. She secured the tray on a shelf in the walk-in fridge, then backed out and shut the door. She stepped towards the entryway to the front of the bakery and took in a deep breath before pushing through the swinging door to the front area.

"Laura—hello, again," the man said, as she pushed open the door.

Laura stopped in the doorway holding the swinging door wide. With her other hand, she lifted a corner of her apron to dab at the sweat on her brow, then she brushed back the strands of her hair that had come lose from her bun. "Proff—Christian?" she said, surprised and confused, wiping her hands on the front of her apron. "We're closed... I just forgot to lock the door—we close at 4 p.m. on Sunday."

"Oh," he said, still standing there.

Her exhaustion had hit a breaking point about twenty minutes ago, and now the unease she was experiencing was causing her stomach to flip-flop and she suddenly felt nauseous. She was the only one left in the bakery. "Was there something... else, I could help you with?" She remained in the doorway, only the cash-counter and the display fridge separating them.

"I didn't realize I had missed my opportunity before the closing." He glanced around the shop and then to the empty display area.

Laura stood there still holding the swinging door open, unsure what to do or even what to say. She could feel the sweat building on her upper lip.

"You told me I should pick up some dessert... something *light*, you suggested." He took a step closer.

"Right—yes, but I'm sorry we're closed, like I said." She glanced over her shoulder to the back kitchen, then glanced back to see he had stepped even closer, close enough that he could reach out and touch the glass of the display cabinet.

He made a grimacing, silly sort-of smile then, and said, "I don't suppose you have anything in the back you can sell me? Or have I truly missed my chance?" He gave a sad smile then like a pouting child.

What the hell was the matter with her? Twenty years of evading a stalker—that's what. She blew out a breath. "Yes— no—of course," she said, feeling foolish once again. "Let me see what I can get for you from the fridge." She turned and stepped back into the baking area, the door hitting her on the butt, giving her a startle as she surveyed the already cleaned baking tables. Then she went to the fridge. Inside she snatched up four of the small lemon filled parcel pastries she *hadn't* ruined this morning. As she shut the fridge door, she heard the bell jingle again and recognized she had better lock the door after Christian was gone. She quickly placed the delicate pastries into a decorative light blue gift box with the bakery logo on the top. Then she pushed open the door again, to return to the front area and her unfortunately growing clientele. But the professor was gone, and there was no one else in the store.

Had that jingle been him leaving? "What the…?" she said, to the empty bakery. *The nerve,* she thought, coming in after hours, having her go and get him deserts already put away, for him to serve on his date. She let out a growl of frustration. "What a day," she said, setting the box on the counter to move between the cash and the display case to go lock the door.

She pulled the blind down over the long skinny window of the front door. As she went to turn the lock, the door was suddenly pulled away from her. Laura screamed and shut her eyes, crossing her arms in front of her face. "Stop," a voice said, grabbing her arms, causing Laura to scream again. Laura struggled against the hands holding her arms, then opened her eyes.

"Christian—what the hell?" she said, when she saw who was attempting to restrain her.

"Oh-my-gosh-I'm sorry," he said, finally letting her go. "I just stepped outside to take a call. I am. So. Sorry." He stepped back from her.

"You scared me half to death," Laura scolded, pressing the palms of her hands to her chest, her nerves completely raw now. "Here," she said then, turning back to the counter to grab up the box of pastries. She held them out in front of him.

He stared at the box. "Oh, I couldn't," he said, lifting his hands up as if she were pointing a gun at him. "It was such a bother."

"No. It wasn't. You just frightened me, is all." Laura gave the box a light shake. "Please, just take them. I'm sorry—I've just had a rough 24-hours."

Christian took the box from Laura's hand. "What do I owe you?"

"Nothing—please. Enjoy your dinner date," she breathed out, the rawness of her nerves feeding her exhaustion.

"Thank you, Laura... and I'm sorry for the trouble," he said, backing away and pushing out the door.

She just gave him a wave as she locked the door, she was too tired to do anything more. Then she shut the front area light off, the space still lit by the sun shining in through the large side-window of the bakery. She turned and made her way back to the baking area again, double checking that she had cleaned everything, and that all the perishable foods were safely tucked away in the refrigerators. Then she scooped up her satchel from the office and pulled her phone out to see if Gwen had called back.

There was one message, and she tapped the voicemail button to listen, and hit the speaker option, unsure of what she would hear. *"Mom—Call me back,"* was all there was from her daughter. She had hoped for more, but with her energy stores depleted, she was not sure she could manage the crucial conversation right now.

The phone rang in her hand startling her, taunting her with the urge to throw the thing across the room. The display showed the caller as 'unknown'. Laura had had about enough of the *unknown* to last her a millennium, but in case it was an emergency, she answered. "Yes?"

"Laura?" a woman's voice asked.

"Yes," Laura said, again. "Who is this?"

"It's Marlene—sorry, Hi, I forgot my phone at home, had to call for my messages using a landline. I'm at the university—the student pub, can you meet me here?"

Laura leaned against the nearest baking table. "Sure," Laura said, totally wiped yet still needing to talk to her friend, and the pub was closer—at least, than that restaurant they had met at, so that was good. "I'm at the bakery, so I'll see you in a few."

"Great—see you soon," Marlene said before hanging up.

Laura had never been into the pub though she had passed it on her many walks through the campus. On the way, she considered how odd it was that Marlene was at the pub, especially on a Sunday. What did she care though, she just needed to see her friend.

Laura walked in through the entrance to the pub, it was as she imagined, all dark wood trim and smelling of stale beer. From the entrance hall leading to the main bar area, Laura could see several tables with a scattering of patrons drinking and chatting, though she was unable to see Marlene anywhere. There were several young men at the far side, mingling around a larger table of young women, the men it seemed were taking turns at throwing darts.

She proceeded forward, slowly, noting that the doors to the men's and women's bathrooms were situated midway up the hall, and she was unsure if perhaps she had come in through the wrong entrance. When she got closer to the opening to the main bar, she was relieved to hear Marlene's laughter coming from further down around the corner at the end of the entry hall. Laura smiled at the welcoming sound as she approached, then she stopped a few feet from turning the corner, when she heard Marlene speak.

"She's an interesting case," Laura heard her say. "She thinks we're friends—like our meetings aren't anything other than two friends sitting and talking."

Laura couldn't believe what she was hearing, but despite the words cutting her, she took the last steps forward, showing herself to her so-called friend.

"Hey Laura—you remember...," Marlene started to say.

"I trusted you—I told you things I've never told anyone," Laura said, gripping the purse strap that crossed her chest.

"What? What's wrong?" Marlene said.

As Marlene turned fully towards her, the image of the person Marlene had been speaking to, blurred in Laura's vision. "Have you been analyzing me this whole time? I'd actually thought I'd found a friend, now I find that I've just been another client—unknowingly being analyzed. Doesn't this go against some kind of moral code for practitioners?"

"What are you talking about?" Marlene questioned, bold confusion flooding her face.

"What did you discover—what deep dark secret do you think you've uncovered? That I'm a lonely woman who loves her daughter—more than her own happiness? Was I an interesting case study for you—is that it? Have you lectured about my interesting life, what it means to the psyche—what this does to a child? Or is it all about paranoia and delusions, that you're teaching these days?"

"Why would you think that—we're friends—I don't treat friends," Marlene said.

"Treat—you think I need treatment?" Laura said, throwing her hands in the air.

"No—that's not what I mean," Marlene said.

"'*She's an interesting case—thinks we're friends*'—isn't that what you said to your *colleague* just now?" Laura threw back at her, gripping the strap of her purse again. That was when Laura recognized that the colleague Marlene had been talking to was *Christian*. Laura scowled at both of them.

"I wasn't talking about you—not that it's any of your business, but I was talking about a female police officer client of mine. She's struggling with the idea of needing help, as you can imagine," Marlene said, stepping closer to Laura.

"Right—you think I need help?" Laura stepped back.

"That's not what I mean."

Marlene was getting frustrated now; Laura could see that. *Well join the club*, she thought. "What *do* you mean then?" Laura asked. "Actually—I don't want to know, this whatever-friendship—this is over." Laura shot a glance at Christian. "And you," Laura said, pointing at him, "I hope you choke on that meal." She looked back to Marlene. "I should have known better—trusting people, trusting you. You do not understand what it's like to run for most of your life. To be so broken down that you can't even make friends."

"Please calm down," Marlene said, stepping forward again, this time with her hands up.

"Don't tell me to calm down," Laura shouted. She didn't care about Marlene's colleague standing there, she didn't care about anyone who could hear her. "You think I'm nuts, cuckoo, off my rocker, missing a few marbles, eh?" Laura stepped back away from Marlene again, she didn't want her near her. "Why have I tried so hard all these years to be something I'm not? Why can't I just be me?" Laura turned then and ran back up the hall.

"Laura don't go," she heard Marlene call, as she took off bolting out the door.

Chapter 16

Detective Franklin was relieved to be meeting Gwen at what had become their usual meet-up place, the diner.

Heading in, he spotted her at a booth nearest to the entrance. "Here," he said, as he lowered himself into the seat across from her. "The originals. I made copies for the file—figured you wouldn't mind."

"Coffees?" the waitress asked, setting down another glass of ice water, as per usual.

"Please," he told the woman.

"Yes," Gwen said, "I don't really want the coffee. But I just pulled an 18-hour shift, so I need it. I should eat too; I've barely had anything to eat all day, with the extra shift and being too restless waiting to meet with you." As the waitress filled their cups, Gwen took the letters and shoved them into her knapsack. When the waitress left, she said, "I think my mother and Rachel knew each other—though she denies knowing anything about her or the letters. She left me a message… about my father—that he's not dead—that she'd changed her last name," Gwen blurted, letting out the breath it seemed she'd been holding.

"What—why?" was all he had in return.

"I was told my father was dead, but I think he's the guy who's been following Rachel in those letters—following us, this serial killer you've been tracking. My mother has been keeping us on the move all this time." She took a sip of her coffee and winced. She normally added cream to her coffee he remembered, realizing she must have burned her lip.

"Here—drink this—the ice will help," he said, pushing the glass of water closer to her.

"Thanks. I don't know how you can drink it so hot." She sipped the cold water, letting the ice at the top of the glass rest against her upper lip.

"Practice," he said, and Gwen gave an attempt at a smile. "Did your mother say who your father was?"

"When I was younger, she'd told me his name was 'Frank Jamison', but I'm guessing now that it's a lie too."

"What else?" he pushed. He had been waiting a long time for a break in the case.

"I was already on a call site when she rang me back the first time. I told her to call you." She sipped again. "I called her once more after I heard her message—but got voicemail. I can't believe she kept this from me," she said, letting out a clearly exasperated breath.

"You said you'd never seen the letters before, correct?" he steepled his fingers in front of his coffee cup.

"Ya, I couldn't be sure exactly—but I think they were new to the trunk's contents. There weren't in there before my mother's visit to see my grandmother. She'd been sick—my grandmother, she died actually—but yes, I'd never seen them before that," Gwen said, as if clarifying for him.

He gave her an acknowledging nod. He had reviewed the letters thoroughly, the dates and places, they had all matched up to the reports on the serial killer's movements. But at his previous meet-up with Gwen, he had left out telling her a crucial detail about Rachel's parents, the fact that Rachel's mother had recently been murdered.

"My mother liked to collect textbooks—and there was another book added to the collection in the trunk after that visit to my grandmother, as well," Gwen said. "Written by *Professor Michael Rampton.*"

"That's Rachel's father," he said. "Your mother must know Rachel—and I feel pretty certain she knows who this man is too."

She nodded her understanding at him this time. He watched as she took another sip of water and then began rubbing at her temples.

"Rachel's father was a bad man, Gwen," he said, but he knew she had already figured as much. "Whoever's doing these killings—been following Rachel, possibly stalking your mother and you all these years, maybe this all has something to do with him," he stated.

Gwen pulled something from the front zippered pocket of her knapsack then. "I found a couple photos of my mother in the trunk too," she said, holding what he saw now was a tattered old photo. "But this one, I found it intriguing because I have never seen my mother with her hair down, or wild like this for that matter. It must have been taken before I was born," she said, passing it on over to him.

He stared at the photo, then felt his usual stoic expression shift. It wasn't because he recognized that he knew the girl in the photo, it was because the girl in the photo, was wearing... "My leather jacket," he said, memories flooding through his brain. He flipped the photo over to see a date written on the back. "This was taken a few months after she'd disappeared—after I last saw her." He glanced up at Gwen.

"Yoooour jacket?" Gwen scrutinized, frowning then.

"Rachel and I... we... the last time I saw her... we... she...," he stumbled out.

"Rachel?" Gwen questioned him, her eyes growing wide. "That's my mother."

"What?" he said. In that split-second moment he watched as Gwen's expression changed from surprise suddenly to horror.

"Yer my father—it's you!" she shouted, grabbing her knapsack, squirming out of her seat in the booth.

Speechless, he turned to watch as she pushed through the café door and then dash out of sight.

He had not understood her initial reaction, but then a unique kind of clarity had hit him. *Gwen thinks you're her father*, he'd grasped, though her face shifting to that harrowed expression had clearly said… *you're a murderer*. What was also clear to him now, was where Gwen would be heading… *to her mother's*.

Chapter 17

Questions and panic spun in Gwen's head the whole train ride out to Ann Arbor. She had almost wrenched her neck from checking back over her shoulder to see if he had followed her. She was running on adrenaline now, horribly aware that not only was her father alive, he was the detective she had trusted, her friend's father, and was this serial killer who had terrorized Rachel and more than likely her mother for the past 20 years.

After the fiftieth check over her shoulder, she was still worried he would catch up to her, but so far, she hadn't seen any sign of him. She had never stated exactly where her mother lived, so he wouldn't know where to find her, Gwen had originally thought, but as she stepped off the train now, into the humid early evening air, a sick realization hit her in her already throbbing brain. *He could find them.* He was a cop; he had the means to look up her mother's address and find her. Gwen retrieved her phone from her knapsack's zippered pouch and then shoved it into her back pocket. Despite being the only person getting off the train at this stop, Gwen kept up with checking over her shoulder as she walked the distance from the station to her mother's home.

Arriving at the house, Gwen called out for her mother, but unfortunately like the previous time she had been there, she heard only the sound of the pumping air conditioner in response. Gwen locked the door behind her, then dashed from the hall into the dining area, dropping her knapsack on the table before reaching the stairwell. Two at a time she sprinted up the flight of stairs to the second floor. Freaked out and off-the-chart impatient, she headed to her mother's bedroom closet, desperate and in search of answers.

Heart pounding in her chest, stomach lurching, Gwen knelt and lifted the lid of the old trunk yet again. She found then that two new books now topped one of the piles. The first was a *Firearms Safety Manual* from some police academy, and the other was a textbook with a title that she recognized, *Atlas of Human Anatomy*, and was a newer version to the one she had had from her first year of college.

Standing then, with the textbook in her hand, she flipped it open to find an owner sticker on its inside cover. "Property of Professor Timothy Armstrong, Biology 101," she read aloud. And it was labeled from the same college she had attended.

Gwen's cell phone hummed in her back pocket. She slid it free and then answered it without looking. "Hello?" she said, hoping it was her mother—finally calling her back.

"Rachel's mother was murdered—same MO as the others," Inspector Franklin's voice boomed in her ear.

Gwen turned then to find her mother standing at the opening to the walk-in closet. "Oh-my-gawd-you-scared-me. What did you do to your hair?" Gwen asked, shaken and stunned by her mother's appearance. Her mother said nothing, only stood there staring blankly back at her. Though her mother's familiar face had eased some of Gwen's panic, it wasn't just her sudden presence in the closet doorway that had startled her, it was her mother's hair that had shocked her. It was out of its usual bun, and it was wild, untamed and it was... *red*, dark russet red. "Why do you have this textbook?" Gwen asked, despite the detective still talking in her ear. "This belongs to that dead biology professor—the one that was just killed."

Her mother's expression shifted then to something reminiscent of anger. But determined to get answers, Gwen turned away to grab up another textbook, her cell phone still pressed to her ear, the detective still prattling on. One-handed, she flipped the next book open, then read aloud the person's name on the inside cover. Continuing, she did the same with the next textbook, then another, and still another. Turning back to glance over her shoulder, Gwen noticed that her mother had stepped closer into the closet. Gwen spun her head back to the trunk grabbing up the last book, the police manual, and inadvertently dropped her cell phone in the process. Ignoring the phone, she opened the cover of the manual to see *Bradly Stinson* written on the inside. She turned back to look at her mother. At least she recognized her as her mother standing next to her, but then a cruel awareness struck her.

Her mother's eyes, they reminded Gwen of that woman she and Scott had transported to the psychiatric hospital. This wasn't her mother. Someone resembling her mother had taken her place she grasped, as Detective Franklin's voice yelled out through the quiet confines of the closet through the fallen cell phone. Gwen bent reaching for her phone just as a buzzing-snap sounded from behind her. Then a stinging sensation shuddered painfully through her body as she crumpled to the floor of the closet, cell phone just out of reach. She made an agonizing attempt to lift her head and reach for the phone, just as the surface of a large book swung down into her view.

Chapter 18

Gwen awoke on the floor of the closet, with the side of her head throbbing and the nasty scent of the old carpet permeating through her nasal passages. She could see her cell phone near her right hand, and she moved her arm to reach for it only to find that something had been tucked into the crook of her elbow. Gwen pushed herself up from the floor to a sitting position and the something fell.

It was an envelope, though nothing was written on the front. She reached for it, then stopped, listening. She listened carefully then for any sounds in the house, but she could hear only the sound of her own breathing. She held her breath and waited a moment, listening intently again.

Nothing.

Nothing other than the sound of the A/C unit pumping. Breathing a sigh of relief, she leaned her back against the door jamb, then glanced around the closet. Near the open trunk, lay the textbook that had been written by *Professor Michael Rampton*, but the weathered belt that had been wrapped around it, was no longer there. She shuddered, then reached again for the envelope.

Despite there being no name or address, the envelope itself resembled the others, like the ones Rachel had sent to her mother.

It was only when Gwen opened it, then drew out and unfolded the papers, that she saw that this one had been addressed 'Dear Gwen'. She read the first paragraph then paused. That first letter, the single-page letter Rachel had written about her parents, it had mentioned the abuse, the beatings, and that she'd had to leave town, and this one mentioned the same things, but unlike that letter, this one wasn't about Rachel, it was about Rachel *and* Laura, and it was several pages long. She read the first paragraph again.

> Dear Gwen,
> I wrote you this letter to make sure you knew that Laura, that your mother, is with me and that she is safe, and that there is nothing for you to worry about.

Then she paused again. "Where the hell is my mother?" she asked the universe. Gwen picked up her phone then and dialed her mother. Of course, it went to voicemail. "Mom—where are you? Please call me. I need to talk to you." Then she hung up and began reading again.

> I also wanted you to understand what has truly been happening, since I realize now that you have read all my letters, the ones I had written to my mother.
> You know now about the abuse I suffered at the hands of my father and the neglect from my mother, and it is true that I had to endure the sexual depravities of my father as a small child, but when Laura came along, I knew I had to protect her, protect her from my father.

They're sisters, they must be, Gwen thought.

> I let Laura believe that she was loved by him and made sure she was never aware of the abuse he had put upon me, and as a teen, I made sure I was the only one who took the beatings. I had told Laura, that our mother was mean to her because she was jealous of how much my father loved Laura and that they both loved books so much. We were both good in school though

my mother said she didn't think we were very smart. I had protected Laura all those years in that house, but I knew we had to get out of there. I had reported the beatings thinking I had bided us some time but when that failed, I had had to make another plan to get us out of town.

I had plenty of money from my earnings to take us far away, but Laura had wanted to go to Hanover, New Hampshire because it had a world-class college and a thriving art community, that Laura had craved. When we got there, Laura signed up for a course in Art History, stating that she had had enough of the intensive subjects such as American history and brain numbing Trigonometry that we had taken in high school, and that she preferred to focus on something creative. The professor teaching the course flirted with the female students and had gotten too friendly with Laura, but I fixed that. I had to protect Laura and those other women he was fraternizing with. Laura hadn't been able to finish her course obviously and since she'd had to borrow a textbook for it, and loved school and learning so much, I took the professor's personal textbook for Laura to keep for herself.

When Laura found she was pregnant, she was in denial saying she didn't know how it could have happened. She claimed she only had a faint recollection of a man but nothing more, but I knew how it had happened.

I had called our mother that same week, and that was when she told me about my father, how she blamed me for his death. I told Laura about the call, but in order to protect her, I had to lie to her and tell her that mother had sent someone after us. That's when I changed our last names, and had showed her how to dye her hair and I had even invented a story about a dead husband she could use if anyone asked about the pregnancy or the baby. Then I told her we needed to leave town, and that our best chance was to split up. I explained to her that I would be watching over her, protecting the two of you now.

We moved to Maine and once again Laura found herself associated with another professor who had a problem with keeping it in his pants. January of the following year Laura had taken a basic computer course in the evenings at Bowdoin College, needing to learn to use the computer at her job, but the gossip around campus was that the Computer Science Professor, Laura's professor, had had an affair with a student, and I would not stand for him going after Laura next. As you know, he ended up dead. And again, I took the class textbook, this one was titled the Computer Science Illuminated.

When we were in Vermont, Laura insisted she take a course in Gender, Sexuality & Feminist Studies at Middlebury College, which I thought would be a good education for her and might empower her more when dealing with these types of men, give her a little more backbone. While in her class, she had unfortunately had a run-in with the professor who taught Comparative Literature, a card-member-holding misogynist, who had made some vulgar remarks about Feminism. As you know, my father was a professor of Literature and he had felt the same way about a woman's place in the world. So clearly this professor too needed to be dealt with, and was found dead in the Gender, Sexuality & Feminist Studies meeting room. Which I thought was a nice touch. And I took his Comparative Literature textbook as well.

Six months later we were in Clinton, NY, and Laura had gotten a job as a baker owned by a nice Spanish couple, and she had wanted to learn to speak Spanish, to better communicate with the other bakers and cooks who spoke very little English. She signed up for a class at Hamilton College but instead of learning some words and phrases to help her at work, she had ended up with another lech of a professor who hit on all the female students, not just Laura, offering extra credit for private study sessions. She left the class, and quit her job, and we moved. The professor had been dealt with, and I took his textbook, the Living Language Complete Edition, in fact. Laura just couldn't stomach being around the other Spanish-speaking men, a constant reminder of that professor.

We moved to Lewisburg next, stayed for a year without any issues, until that asshole Professor of Food Systems had come into Laura's work and mouthed off. The food at the bakery was amazing and Laura was an amazing baker, but he still made negative remarks about the place despite eating there every day. He was taken care of, but Laura had gotten questioned by the local police along with the other staff, so to avoid any suspicion, we'd stayed for a year there before moving on. I did get Laura a nice textbook though, the Introduction to Food Science and Food Systems. No harm in learning more about food.

Next, we moved to Maryland, it was very nice, and the Notre Dame of Maryland University was beautiful. The school offered Maryland's only women's college, with programs to help prepare students for leadership and success. We stayed there for two years before any more trouble came our way.

Laura was taking a course in business, recommended and paid for by her new boss, who had wanted someone to help run the place, not just doing the baking. It was a great opportunity, but on the nights she took her class, she had seen female students coming and going from the office of the Professor of international Business—a different female student each time, always fixing their clothes and hair or whatever. On the last night of her course, she had seen one come out crying. That professor gotten what he deserved, and Laura, she was made manager at the bakery and we had ourselves a nice textbook on International Business: Competing in the Global Marketplace. But we left the following year.

We liked the towns that had renowned schools, like the University of Virginia in Charlottesville. We were there for a year when Laura decided she wanted to expand her cooking knowledge and the school had offered government funded cooking classes in the evenings. It had been a pretty intensive class for Laura, but she had loved it. Though, on the last day, when she and her classmates had been celebrating with a holiday meal they'd prepared, Laura had crossed paths with the

Professor of The Politics of Food. He seemed to think men were better cooks than woman, but fortunately or unfortunately— for him, his last meal had been one prepared by Laura and her classmates. Laura got another nice textbook out of it, and she went on to help develop a new line for the bakery which she ran for two years before we move to Asheville, North Carolina.

Laura worked for a catering company there for two years, and during that time the company often provided their food services at the university for department functions. But it was at the university's Engineering Department's function that things went bad. There was a visiting professor at the event, and apparently he was not well-liked, another typical misogynist who felt he had to tell the female engineers at the event it was a man's world and there was no place for women in the engineering field, but they were 'welcome to play in it'. No one seemed to mind it when they heard he'd been killed, and he wouldn't miss the textbook I took, the Fundamentals: An Introduction.

We were off again shortly after that, to West Virginia and Laura was at yet another job, this one at a bakery/supermarket. She had wanted to better herself further and had signed up for an accounting class at the local university. She had been thinking that maybe she could get a manager job and help run the place. As long as Laura was happy, I was all for it. The only male professor in that department was an old guy who really didn't teach and had young male teaching assistant do all the work. Surprisingly though, Laura told me later that the old professor was a bit of a lech, and she and the other female students tried their best to avoid him. He'd come into the class spouting ignorant things like how women were not good at math, that they had computers to do all the work for them. Apparently, he had tenure there, and because he was hated so much, when he'd been found dead, some of the professors had been under suspicion since the old guy's spot on the faculty would be up for grabs. We stayed in town for a while since the cops didn't seem involved in investigating. Then when some visiting detective from Detroit had come to town, we'd heard on the radio that despite the guy being 80, his murder had the same MO, and we were gone again after that. I did get Laura a nice textbook on Accounting Principles that she could use though.

We didn't make it very far that time, only as far as Ohio. You had gotten sick, some kind of stomach issue. We had to stay for a bit and Laura had to get some crap job to pay the medical bills since she had no insurance. That pathetic excuse for a doctor/professor kept saying your pain was all in your head. That failure of a human being only taught one class at Kenyon College, an intro class in child psychology but he thought he knew it all. He was the one who needed his head examined, but his textbook, that information in it was interesting I have to say, plus, it gave us an excuse to get out of that town as fast as we could.

We stayed for two years next in Greencastle, you were young then and probably don't remember that, but you were doing well there, healthy and enjoying school. The university there had a pretty extensive art program and Laura signed up for an art class, no theory, just some drawing and painting. But as par for the course, there was another sicko of a professor at this university as well. This Professor of Film Studies was a real doozy too. A video he had made had gotten out, one of him with a female student where he'd tied her up and he'd threatened her not to tell anyone. That had been the end of his film career, but the textbook he used for his class had some fascinating stuff about movies I'd never seen.

Gwen didn't remember much any of it, not really. There were patchy memories of moving, and different houses and schools, and of course she recalled when she had gotten sick, but she hadn't kept track of the all the cities. The thing she remembered the most about those years, was how much she hated the moving.

You'll probably remember this next move, because you and Laura took a summer course on Nutrition and Healing with Food at Eastern Illinois University. I'm not sure if you would remember this other professor, the one who taught Sports Nutrition, but he was another know-it-all who thought doctors were all idiots. When he got wind of why you and Laura were in the class, he felt he needed to tell you what was what, but everything he had said was the opposite to what you'd learned in the course and what the doctors had said to Laura. He thought he knew all about eating healthy, but healthy didn't get you anywhere if someone killed you. I think Laura still has his textbook. I never read it. We had only been in Charleston for the summer when we got the tip to change direction for our next move and that's when we went to Michigan instead of continuing West.

This move, Gwen did remember. It had been eating at her brain since Detective Franklin had mentioned of the murder, and when she'd asked her mother, she confirmed they'd lived there. After that, Gwen had started to have a clearer memory of her mother arguing with some teacher, and she had remembered correctly, and now she even knew why they'd been arguing. She knew a hell of a lot more than she had ever expected to know now, most of it she wished she didn't, or at a minimum, wished was not true.

It hadn't been easy, and I managed to keep the two of you safe, but each move we made, every town we went to, there always seemed to be some professor, some man who made our lives difficult. And in order to keep Laura from going to the cops and to keep her moving when I needed her too, I had to come up with an idea to keep control of things. So, I played on the idea about someone being after us, by leaving her postcards with directions to stay or move, warnings to stay away from the police, and threats on her life if she didn't comply. She burned each of them of course, which was good. We didn't need that kind of evidence around.

Those letters that I sent to my mother, were with the hopes of convincing her I was in danger of being killed, but she only ever read the first, she obviously didn't care what happened to me.

I'm confident by now, you understand what I was really doing, that I wasn't running from a serial killer, that I killed all of them, all of those professors, all of those vile men, the ones that Laura never seemed to be able to escape. Laura never knew it was me all these years. Although I may have gotten it wrong with that biology professor at your college, you weren't in danger I know that now, and though he wasn't your teacher, he was still being inappropriate with the other female students there. And that cop, Stinson, that one was just for me, he'd had it coming for a long time.

I'm sure you also understand why I did what I did, that I had to protect her, but none of us can be fully protected until I take care of the last two evil men on my list. Once I do, we will all finally be safe.

~ Rachel

What other men? Why did she need to keep killing—why was this even an option, how had Rachel rationalized that it was their only option and why the hell had she taken her mother with her? How was this keeping her mother safe? Gwen's head ached from the injury, and from all the questions, old and new, that thrummed through her brain.

Gwen checked her phone for the time, and it showed it was 6 o'clock, so she hadn't been out for long. But her phone also showed ten missed calls and several messages from both Detective Franklin and Scott. She didn't check the messages, she already knew she had plenty of explaining to do, and she hit dial on Detective Franklin's number to do so.

"What happened—what took you so long to get back to me?" Detective Franklin's voice boomed, much too loud for Gwen's paining head.

Gwen looked at the time on her phone again. Apparently, she had been out cold for more than a few minutes, as it wasn't 6 p.m.

Sunday, it was Monday, and it was now morning. "Well... I got knocked out." She touched the side of her head and face where she'd been hit. She winced and felt a nice hematoma forming on her head near her hairline.

"What—are you okay?" the detective's voice said, booming in her ear again.

"Yes—I'm fine," Gwen said, softly, hoping to lead by example.

"Where are you?" he said, worry still sounding in his voice.

"I'm at my mother's house," she said.

"Where is your mother—is she with you, is she okay?"

"No, yes, I mean no—she's not with me, but I believe she's okay, she's with Rachel."

"Rachel? What are you talking about?" the detective asked, his voice rising again.

"I don't think she would hurt her, though. Rachel's been protecting my mom for a long time, protecting both of us," Gwen said, leaning her head against the jamb and closing her eyes.

"Protecting you?"

"Look, I'm fine. If she had wanted to kill me, she probably could have—but didn't." Gwen went on to explain what had happened to her, about Rachel being here and knocking her out, and about the *letter* that had been left for her.

"I can't believe it—all these years, it's been *Rachel* I've been trying to find. Do you have any idea where she and your mother may have gone?"

"If they are still in town—the college, maybe. There was a lot in the letter about the universities and my mother loves to walk the campuses, but that's my best guess," she said, shifting to her knees to get up.

"I'll contact the local police there and have them send out some officers to check it out," the detective said, his voice calmer now.

"I don't think my mom is in any danger. After reading that letter—I can't imagine Rachel would do anything to my mother." Gwen's head spun then, and she sat back down on the floor. "But I don't know who Rachel was talking about with regards to these other two men," she said, leaning back against the doorframe into the closet.

"I think I do," he said, followed by what sounded to Gwen like a car door slamming.

"Are you sure you're okay—can I send someone over there?" he asked her.

"No—I'm a paramedic, I know how to take care of a bump on the head. But can you let Scott know where I am and explain that I'm okay, and that I won't be able to work today? I'll text you the address here, so you have it." She heard a car engine start and rev then.

"Okay, and yes—of course. Scott has been worried about you too. He'll be glad to hear you are alright and don't worry about your shift."

"Thank you—and oh-my-god—I'm so sorry for thinking you were a serial killer," Gwen said, the queasiness of it all washing over her.

"Gwen, I completely understand the confusion—I'm just glad you're okay," he said, gentle sincerity reaching through the phone to her.

"This is all such a lot to digest," she said, swallowing down her headache nausea.

"We're going to figure this all out and find your mom. And these men Rachel mentioned, if they are who I think they are— I'm going to need to get some surveillance on them. Let me get on it—I'll keep you posted," the detective said, the car engine sound revving again.

"Thank you, Detective," she said before hanging up.

Gwen put down her phone on the letter from Rachel, and then glanced around the closet again. On the other side of the trunk she saw that there was a pile of clothing and a pair of what looked like men's work-boots.

Gwen shifted to her knees again, then crawled over to the pile where she found a man's coat, pants, and shirt. Under the coat she discovered gloves, a hat, and a dark-haired wig and fake beard, *and* she was fully cognizant that this was the clothing worn by the serial killer in the videos Detective Franklin had mentioned. Gwen also knew whoever these two men were that Rachel had written about at the end of her letter, the ones she'd stated she was going to *take care of*, were going to meet Rachel, and without her disguise this time.

Chapter 19

"Okay Miss Paramedic, time to get yourself up off this floor and check out your injury," Gwen said to herself, as she pulled her unsteady body up from the rough carpet to maneuver out of the closet and into the cooler space of her mother's bedroom. Steadier now, she crossed the short distance to the tiny en-suite bathroom.

In the bathroom, she filled the cup her mother kept next to the sink with water and gulped it back. Placing the cup back, she leaned in and squinted, checking the discolouration on the side of her face and the goose-egg on her head at her hairline. She turned her head to check the other side, and there were no cuts or bleeding that she could see. Then she pulled open the medicine cabinet mirror to locate the aspirin her mother readily kept there. Finding the bottle, she snatched it up and then shut the cabinet. She filled the cup again and downed two tablets with the water, then shoved the pill bottle in her front pocket and maneuvered out of the bathroom back to the closet.

Thankfully, the nausea and the dizziness Gwen had been feeling earlier was beginning to dissipate, and she bent and retrieved the letter. She made her way out of the bedroom, into the second-floor hallway, and then down the stairs. On the main floor, as she set the letter next to her knapsack, the sun was attempting to pierce through the curtains on the far side of the living room, as morning showed itself and what was potentially going to be another scorcher of a day.

Gwen went to the kitchen, then at the counter she spread out one of the dishtowels that her mother had stacked there. Then she took a tray of ice cubes from the freezer and twisted it, cracking the cubes loose over the dishtowel. Securing the corners of the towel together in a bunch, she lifted the homemade cold pack to her paining head, and then leaned against the counter.

The cooling sensation felt soothing against the bump on her head, and she was hopeful the ice would ease further swelling. The side of her face, on the other hand, was in store for an even nastier bruise than what she'd already seen reflected in the mirror, and would go through a series of colour changes over the next few days, giving her a similar appearance to that of a sucker-punched boxer.

Her stomach grumbled and she grasped that it had been almost a day since she had eaten anything, and that this state of hunger coupled with the sluggishly dissolving headache was not the condition she needed to be in if she was to support the detective in finding her mother. She went back to the fridge and in it she found a container of her mother's macaroni salad, and just what she needed, delicious and no need to heat it. Placing the dishtowel icepack back on the counter, Gwen took the food from the fridge, and a fork from the silverware drawer, and then went and to the dining table to eat. She shoved her knapsack to the side and sat down. But as soon as she did, there was a *Knock-Knock* at the front door.

Gwen set down her fork and got up from the table and headed down the hall to the front door. "Who is it," she said, out of habit, then she unlocked and opened the door before waiting for a reply.

The morning air was already warming, and Gwen felt a hit of queasiness surface up in her. A towering woman with light-blond hair pulled back in a bun, and wearing a navy-blue maxi-dress, stood smiling at her from the front step. Before Gwen could say anything, the woman said, "You must be Gwen—your mother has told me all about you."

"And you are?" Gwen asked, less polite under the circumstances than she normally would have been.

"Oh, I'm sorry—I'm Dr. Marlene Branden, I'm a friend of your mother's." She tried to look around Gwen down the hall.

"She's not here right now—is there something I could help you with?" Gwen asked, not remotely in the mood to chat with one of her mother's friends. She didn't even know her mother had any friends.

"Do you know when she'll be back—I really need to speak with her?" the tall doctor asked her. Then the woman frowned and tilted her head to stare at the obvious bruise and bump on the side of Gwen's head. "My dear—are you okay—that's a nasty injury you have there, would you let me take a look at that?"

Gwen took in a long drawn out breath, then exhaled. She wasn't okay and it wasn't because of the whack she'd taken to the head. Surrendering to the idea of aid, Gwen said, "You might as well come in—I don't know when my mother will be back but, maybe you could help with that." If they were friends, this woman might have a better idea where she and the detective might find her. Plus, Gwen knew it was better to not be alone with a head injury even though she had told the detective she was fine and for him not to worry.

"Have you already had this checked out," the doctor asked, following as Gwen led them to the dining area.

Gwen sat back down in her chair. "Ya—I checked it out. Looks worse than it is I think," Gwen told the doctor as she pulled out a chair to sit down.

Before sitting she said, "Right—paramedic. Have you used some ice on it?"

Gwen pointed over to the counter where her poorly made icepack lay melting on the counter.

Instead of sitting, the doctor went to the kitchen counter and swiftly drew together the corners of the dishtowel, then twisted the fabric and secured the ice into a bunch. Returning to the table, she handed Gwen the ice pack. "Here," she said, "might be best to keep that against your head a bit longer." She grinned at Gwen and the woman's cheeks bunched.

"How do you know my mother?" Gwen asked then, placing the cold, now damp towel to the side of her head.

"We met a few years back near the campus where I teach— we were both out on work breaks, sitting on one of those public benches, and we got to chatting—the rest is history, I guess you could say." She grinned again.

"Why are you here—what did you need to talk to her about?"

The doctor's smile dropped, and she said, "Well—we had a misunderstanding last night—and had a pretty nasty blow-up." She breathed out and her shoulders sagged. "I'm worried about her actually—she didn't return any of my texts and isn't answering my calls." She set her shoulder bag on the table then. "I know you and I haven't met before, but I'm assuming your mother told you about me and our meetups, no?"

"No," Gwen said, "Sorry—do you mind if I eat? I haven't eaten since Sunday morning."

"My gosh—of course," the doctor said. "Was that injury from on the job?" She tilted her face to look at the side of Gwen's head again.

"Uhm, no—it's a long story," Gwen said, then shoveled the cold pasta into her mouth and chewed.

"Well, your mother and I have been meeting for coffee and pastries religiously, for over three years now, and we've become close—at least I thought we had." She sat back in her chair and folded her hands in her lap, then said, "Your mother is smart and caring... and I thought we could both use some girlfriend time— you know what I mean, get out for dinner or drinks. But I was afraid to push too hard, thought I might scare her away—she's like a frightened mouse, and had only now really started to open up to me more and she had agreed to come out."

Gwen gave a nod, but said nothing, continuing to chew her food and listen, as her mother's friend went on to explain their friendship.

"I'm not a social butterfly—but I enjoy getting out some, I'm usually curled up reading a good book or watching a good movie most nights, and with your mother—I believed there's a great woman in there dying to get out and have some fun—you know?"

Gwen nodded again.

"I was very patient with her and finally asked her to go out— I wanted to show her it was safe. It's all about trust with her and I was fairly confident you would have liked for her to get out and have some fun—she had alluded to it at times."

"Did you guys end up going out?"

"Yes—just the other night in fact, and we had fun—she had fun. But I know there is more going on with her. I believe in honesty between friends and colleagues, so was hoping she could be honest with me, but I find myself tending to treat her like a patient—she troubles me sometimes. I get that your mother's situation is complicated."

"What kind of doctor are you?" Gwen asked.

"I'm a psychologist—I have a small practice out of my home, but I also teach at the university." The doctor leaned a forearm on the dining table.

"Well, my mother is a lot more complicated than I realized," Gwen said, leaning her elbows on the table, icepack still against her head. "I'd told her once that she needed to see someone about her paranoia. She told me she was seeing a psychologist, but I hadn't realized it was more of a friend thing. She had seemed so much better, more relaxed, so I figured the sessions were helping her. Guess she lied about the sessions, hoping to ease my worries over her. It worked, but," Gwen said, with a defeated shrug.

"Did your mother ever tell you about why she had to move you guys around so much?"

"I didn't know at the time, but I do now," Gwen said, leaning back in her chair and setting the mostly melted icepack on the table next to the food empty container.

"So, you've read the letter from her, about why you moved so much... about the stalker?"

"She told you about the stalker?" Gwen asked, her eyes going wide.

"Yes—but she only just told me about it the other day. She'd said she was going to write out everything in a letter—and give it to you."

"My mother never gave me a letter, but Rachel left me one. I've read all of Rachel's other letters too."

"Who's Rachel? And what other letters?" The doctor frowned.

"Wait—if you knew about the stalker—how do you not know about Rachel?"

"Like I mentioned, your mother had only just started to open up and had finally unburdened herself to me about this man, the one whose been following her across the country—this stalker."

"Oh boy—okay, ya there's a lot more you don't know. There was a lot I didn't know until just this morning, actually," Gwen rushed out. Then she did her best to give the doctor the details on Rachel's letters and the last 24-hours. "I didn't understand why my mother had the letters—I didn't realize who Rachel was. The letters made it sound like someone was after Rachel—a man that Rachel believed was a serial killer. When I questioned my mother, she denied knowing anything about Rachel or the letters. I had told her she needed to talk to Detective Franklin—he's the lead on the serial killer case. She had left me a message after, saying that my father was still alive, that she didn't know his name—but that he'd raped her and that he was following us— that he was doing these killings. But it's Rachel, she is the killer, not my father."

"Who is this Rachel, do you know?"

"Based on this letter," Gwen slid the new letter across the table. "I'm pretty sure she's my mother's sister. Older sister, I think. Rachel mentions in the letter, 'when Laura came along' like as if she had been born after Rachel. It better explains the photos I found too. They look so much alike they could be twins."

Dr. Branden started reading the letter then stopped. "Do you have the photos here?" she asked looking up at Gwen, then she returned to reading the letter.

"Just the one—Detective Franklin has the other one." Gwen reached for her knapsack and pulled the photo from the zippered pouch and handed it to the doctor. "That's my mother and me," Gwen said when the doctor glanced up from reading.

"She looks very happy here." She smiled at Gwen. "I've never seen any photos of you as a baby. I've only ever seen the ones your mother keeps on her phone from your high school graduation."

"I have only seen few of the earlier photos myself," Gwen shared, a hint of melancholy in her voice.

"If it was Rachel doing this, and not your father? Where is he—your mother told me, he died?"

"I have no idea. I came here last night to confront my mother about my father, but she wasn't here. She must have been with you. I had thought both photos were of my mother, so when Detective Franklin recognized his jacket in that one photo—

Rachel was wearing it in the photo, I thought it was him—that he'd raped her, that he was the serial killer. I ran out of the diner before he could explain. I was obviously wrong about that— major mix-up—he's from their hometown, he knew Rachel, but not my mother." Gwen shook her head.

A firm *Knocking* sounded from the front door. "That's probably Detective Franklin," Gwen said, setting the icepack down and getting up to answer the door. Gwen noticed then that she hadn't locked the door, so she just turned the knob and pulled it open.

A waft of hot summer air hit Gwen as she pulled open wide the door to find a worried and sweaty-faced Detective Franklin standing in front of her. "Hey—oh dear—that looks like a nasty hit you took there," the detective said, wincing and stepping into the front hall, when Gwen stepped back. "Did you put any ice on it?"

"Already on it," Gwen said. "Dr. Marlene Branden—this is Detective Jim Franklin," Gwen added, introducing her mother's friend, as she and the detective came into the dining area. The doctor set the letter aside and smiled up at the detective.

"Dr. Branden?" Detective Franklin said, looking from her to Gwen.

"Marlene—please. I'm a good friend of Gwen's mother," she said, as if hoping to clear up the detective's confusion, standing then and putting out a hand.

Detective Franklin gave her a smile then shook her hand, and then looked to Gwen again.

"She's a psychologist—works at the university too. She knew about the stalker, but…," Gwen started to say.

"But Gwen has caught me up on everything," Marlene added for Gwen.

"You can talk in front of her—like she said, she knows it all now."

"Okay," he said.

"Here have a seat," Gwen said, pulling out another chair at the table, before sitting down again herself.

Dr. Branden gathered up the soggy dishtowel mess off the table then and went to the sink. "Gwen, does your mother have any resealable plastic bags?"

"Second drawer," she said, then turned back to the detective. "Do you have any updates on my mother?"

"I'm afraid not—but there's been another murder."

"Was it one of the men you thought Rachel might be after?" Gwen asked.

"Yes—Robert Thompson, another past associate of my father's. He was the other officer on site at the police station when Rachel had come in and made her report all those years ago. He had moved here shortly after Stinson. He was working as a beat cop—but he messed up and lost his job. We found him at his current job—same MO. The body was found next to the security booth in a pay-to park, parking garage in downtown Detroit."

Dr. Branden returned to the table with a freshly made icepack of what was basically frozen peas in a resealable plastic bag. "Here—put this against your head," she told Gwen, then sat back down into her seat.

"Are you okay—maybe you should get that checked out," the detective said.

"She'll be fine. I'm a medical doctor too—I just did my residency in psych." She grinned at the detective.

"Do you have that photo, the one of Rachel?" Gwen asked the detective, redirecting all the quasi parental concerns.

"Yes," the detective said, pulling his wallet from his back pocket. He slid the photo from the bill fold and handed it to Gwen.

"See here Dr. Branden, this one is of Rachel." Gwen put the photo of her and her mother next to it.

"Detective, this is the letter from Rachel—you're going to want to read that." Dr. Branden said, tapping the stack of stapled pages in front of her.

"It's pretty evident in the letter that my mother and Rachel are sisters," Gwen said, sliding the photos over for the detective to see.

Detective Franklin glared down at the photos, then said, "Rachel didn't have a sister; she didn't have any other siblings in fact."

"That can't be right," Gwen said, frowning.

"When Rachel had disappeared—and then her father had been killed in that car crash, the police had gone to Rachel's house to speak to the mother. They did a thorough investigation, and there were definitely no other children living in that house. Rachel had been their only child.

Gwen shook her head and closed her eyes. Her headache was returning. "I don't understand," she said, pulling the aspirin bottle from her pocket and dispensing two of the tablets onto her palm.

"May I see the other letters from Rachel?" Dr. Branden asked then.

Gwen took out the letters from her knapsack and handed the stack to Dr. Branden, before getting up to get some water to take the pills. Returning to the table, Gwen and the detective watched as she opened and scanned through each of the single-page letters.

"I think I understand what has been going on." Dr. Branden glanced up at the detective. "Are you sure you are ready for this?" she asked, turning to look directly at Gwen.

Chapter 20

Gwen had not been ready for this, not any of it, and she still had mostly questions, but there were three things she was now positive about, and largely because Dr. Branden had taken the time to explain it all.

First, her mother Laura, Gwen knew without a doubt, was in fact *Rachel*.

Secondly, she/they, from what Dr. Branden had described, suffered from what was known in her professional circles as, *Dissociative Identity Disorder*, but more commonly known as split personality.

Gwen had felt it also explained a lot about her mother's conduct and the things that she had done over the years, those things that had stuck out as odd to her. Gwen had known that her mother worried over *something*, but she had not been aware of what it was, and the behaviors her mother had displayed, she had assumed were just your typical weird parental behaviors. Gwen had known her childhood was not a normal one, but they had been happy for the most part, made the best of things, and her mother had been a wonderful mom, taking good care of her. Her mother had even agreed to stay in Ann Arbor when Gwen had begged her.

This disorder, the condition, that her mother had been suffering from, also explained the photos, and how they could have looked so much alike, but still different at the same time. The first photo of the young woman in the leather jacket, the one Detective Franklin had identified as Rachel, had been taken soon after they had met, and the photo showed her with a joyful yet mischievous smile that hinted of a fiercer side, where the photo of Gwen as a baby with her mother, showed a more passive plain version of the woman Gwen knew as her mother. Detective Franklin had confirmed that Rachel had dark red hair, but it was obvious to Gwen now, that her mother had been dying hers and passing it off as a need to cover early grey, as her mother had told her. They were the same person, but the difference in their personalities shone through in those photos.

Dr. Branden had explained that Rachel must have suffered a traumatic mental break at some point causing the split, and had considered perhaps it had happened during Rachel's early childhood of abuse, but she had said she couldn't be more precise with the age without further observation and discussion with both personalities. Gwen understood her mother needed help, psychological help, and it was painfully obvious what Rachel, what her *mother*, had been doing all these years. Rachel may have been protecting Laura and Gwen, but sadly, she had also been killing people in the process.

And the *third* thing, that Gwen knew for certain, was that Detective Franklin had been the man chasing after—following Rachel and following her mother and Gwen from state to state, yet not in the way it had been portrayed or interpreted by Rachel/them of course. And as part of this certainty, Gwen understood now what Rachel had meant in her letter by 'she knew' regarding how Laura had gotten pregnant. It hadn't been that professor, and it hadn't been rape. It had been Rachel's one night of *no commitment* with Jamie that had indirectly created a *lifetime* commitment of parenthood for Laura, and that Jim Franklin was most certainly, *her father.*

Gwen also understood that with the help from both Dr. Branden—her mother's only friend, and Detective Franklin— Gwen's real father, that working together with them, was the only way they were going to find Rachel, and with any luck, keep her from committing another murder. But right now, along with finding Rachel, the main thing Gwen was focused on was making sure that in the end, her mother—Laura, would get the help she ultimately needed.

The detective had felt it best that Gwen come with him to the station, safer perhaps, not that he believed Rachel would kill her, but the last thing she needed, was another blow to the head. Dr. Branden had called and rearranged her patient meetings to free up her time and had asked to come along and help them with assessing the potential danger Rachel might be willing to put herself in. And they had stopped by Gwen's apartment on the way so she could clean up and get a change of clothing quickly, before proceeding to the station.

"You said a stressor can trigger a change in personality, in motivation of one or more of the personalities?" Detective Franklin asked the doctor once they were all seated in his office.

"Yes, but the one personality—Rachel, has been dormant for six years it seems, so there must have been another trauma or stressor recently that may have set off Rachel's motivation to commit these new murders," Dr. Branden clarified.

"Could I have been the stressor—with my confronting her?" Gwen asked, looking at her phone for the umpteenth time, checking in vain to see if her mother had possibly messaged her.

"Actually, I believe *I* may have been the trigger to the change—the switch up of the personalities, with that fight we had," Dr. Branden said, setting her shoulder bag on her lap. "She had come to meet me yesterday at the college pub, to talk, and it's my understanding, that she must have overheard me talking about one of my patients to a colleague—she had thought I'd been talking about her. She thought I'd been analyzing her all this time—that we weren't really friends," she explained.

"That professor from your school, Gwen, that murder was not as a result of anything either of you did—that happened before either of your conversations with her," the detective stated. "I believe Rachel is wrapping up things, killing all those who she believes could potentially hurt Laura and Gwen, as well as those who had hurt her before, like her mother, and the two officers, Stinson and Thompson, who had not believed her, about what she had told them about the abuse." Detective Franklin leaned forward placing his forearms on his desk, steepling his fingers.

"But Rachel's letter stated she had two more men she needed to take care of? Who's the last man?" Gwen questioned him.

"I'm pretty confident she's after my father now," Detective Franklin said, pulling in a deep breath.

"Your father?" Gwen said, frowning.

"Yes—my father, he'd been the police chief at the time when Rachel had come in. I'd been there at the station, like I told you—that's when I met Rachel. He was a good cop—but he had been a son-of-a-bitch and a hard-ass of a father, and he had been horrible to Rachel that day. He had also believed what her parents had said about her bad behavior despite the terrible injuries she'd had." The muscles of the detective's jaw tensed, and he ran a hand across it as if trying to calm the enraged memory of that day.

"Where is he—your father?" Dr. Branden asked him.

"He's safe. I've sent an officer over to keep a watch on him," the detective said. "He lives in a private retirement center for seniors with Alzheimer's. My mother died ten years ago from cancer—he thinks she's still alive—she'd been a nurse, so he mixes her up with the nurses. They have staff to keep residents in and unwelcome visitors out too though.

"Who would have of thought you'd have to protect your father from a woman he'd once pissed off when she was only eighteen years old," Dr. Branden said, just as the detective's office door opened.

"Sir—sorry to interrupt—but dispatch is having trouble reaching the officer on site at your father's facility," the twenty-something police officer said, leaning into the office still holding onto the doorknob.

At that, Detective Franklin was out of his chair and heading out the open door of his office. Both Gwen and Dr. Branden followed as the detective and the junior officer headed to dispatch.

"What's happening officer?" Detective Franklin demanded.

"Sir—I can't reach Officer Reynolds on his radio," the dispatcher said, covering the mic part of his headset.

"Did you try the front desk at the facility—never mind—I'm heading over there," the detective said, before the dispatcher could respond.

"I'm coming with you," Dr. Branden said, wide-eyed and clutching her shoulder bag tight to her body. "I can help."

"Me too," Gwen added, staring back at the detective. "She's my mother."

"Fine!" he said, turning and heading to the doors to the precinct's parking area.

When they pulled up to the facility, Detective Franklin was out of the car, slamming the door, and already heading up to the main entrance before Gwen and Dr. Branden had even had a chance to get out, and they only caught up with him at the front desk.

When the reception nurse hung up the phone, the detective quickly asked, "Where is Officer Reynolds?"

"Oh, he's such a lovely young man," the chubby-faced nurse started to say.

"Where is he?" the detective asked again, pulling his badge from his belt, flashing it in front of the nurse's face.

"No need to get so huffy," she said. "I saw him about forty-five minutes ago."

The detective spoke then into the handheld radio he had brought with him, "Officer Reynolds—it's Detective Franklin, what is your location?"

No response came through the radio from the detective's attempt to raise this Officer Reynolds on his radio.

"Have you seen this person," Detective Franklin asked the nurse then, pulling a photo from his badge's leather folder.

Gwen leaned around to look at the photo. It was an image from the video footage of Rachel in disguise. "Oh-my-god-I-forgot-to-tell-you—I found the disguise in the closet," Gwen, spewed out, rubbing at the side of her aching head now.

When the detective turned to look at Gwen, the nurse said, "No—no man, but your father's niece is here somewhere."

"What?" Detective Franklin and Gwen shouted at the same time, turning, and staring at the nurse.

"Yes, a lovely redheaded woman. She went to use the ladies' room," the nurse informed them.

"When?" the detective questioned.

"Gee, that was about thirty minutes ago, before I saw the officer doing his checks of the first floor.

"Where is the ladies' room?" Gwen asked.

"Just around the corner, next to the center stairwell," she said, pointing to the left.

Detective Franklin ran to the ladies' room around the corner, with Gwen hot on his heels, but when they entered the bathroom, there was no one in there.

"The stairs," Dr. Branden said, catching up then, indicating the door to the stairwell.

Detective Franklin pulled his service weapon from his belt's holster and then yanked open the door to the stairs. Then holding his gun at his shoulder, he went up the stairs side-stepping with his back to the wall opposite to the side with the open handrail. "Tell the nurse to call for back-up," he said in a hushed voice directed at Dr. Branden. When she nodded, he turned back extending his gun hand, and then edged around the bend in the stairs. Gwen followed him, leaving several steps between them.

At the top of the stairwell on the landing, they found Officer Reynolds. His body was face down, and next to him was what must have been a very large, now smashed vase.

Gwen bent and checked for a pulse. "He's alive—and he's breathing." Gwen glanced up at the detective. "There's a taser burn on his neck."

Detective Franklin bent his gun hand up to his shoulder again, reaching out for the handle to the stairwell's door with his other. Then he pulled it open, pointing his gun out in front of him and checking both ways down the hall. "My father's room is right there," he whispered, pointing to the door opposite and to the left of the stairwell's entrance. Detective Franklin shifted then, crossing the hall to put his back against the wall next to door to his father's room.

Gwen followed again, keeping a short distance between them.

Detective Franklin leaned his ear to the door and silently wrapped his hand around the doorknob.

"Is that you honey? I can't find my glasses," Gwen heard the slightly muffled, yet deep voice of an elderly man say, just before the detective turned the knob.

Detective Franklin burst through, shoving the door wide, his gun in two hands now held out in front of him.

Gwen stood in the doorway, and across from them she could see the back of an old man seated in a chair, facing towards a large window on the opposite wall. Her mother, *Rachel*, stood to the left of the chair, one hand behind her back, the other gripping the ends of what Gwen recognized as the old belt she had seen cinched around that literary textbook. But now it was wrapped around the old man's neck.

"Mom—stop, please," Gwen pleaded.

"Hello, *Dolly*. Sorry, your mother isn't here I'm afraid," Rachel said in response. "Detective Franklin, I presume? How did you like finding your fellow cops that way—or I should say, ex-cops?" Rachel took a quick glance at the old guy. "Oh, and I didn't kill that officer in the hall—he was nice to me."

"You don't have to do this," Detective Franklin said, holding his gun out, pointing it directly at her.

"What? This?" Rachel said, tightening her grip on the belt. "Yes... I do. Just like I had to take care of those other two asshole-cops."

"Your mother didn't just die, did she?" Gwen asked, hoping somehow to reach her mother.

"Nope—I killed the bitch," Rachel said sharply. "She had it coming—just like those two good-for-nothing cops."

"You killed Officer Stinson," Detective Franklin said then.

"Stinson was a gift—for me, actually," Rachel said, producing the taser gun from behind her back. "I'd seen a photo of him and his wife in the newspaper. She's some hotshot lawyer here in Detroit. She's smart—but *ugly*, seems Stinson married someone as ugly as him. The article said something about them selling their big house in that ritzy neighborhood. That's how I found him; hadn't even known he was even in this part of the country."

"They were high school sweethearts," Detective Franklin said, as if trying to appease the Rachel he knew from when they were younger. "She'd come back to our hometown after law school, then moved the two of them here to Detroit."

"Lucky for me, I found him in his car," she said, "holding a rifle. He was about to off himself—but I stopped him. I needed him to tell me where Thompson was now, plus I was curious why he was going to shoot himself. Gambling debts and the wife was divorcing him over it—he said."

"But he did shoot himself," Gwen cut in, still standing in the doorway.

"Ya—I helped him with that. I tasered him first, then wrapped the belt around his neck and choked him until he passed out. I let the shotgun do the rest, but not before I got the details about Thompson, but you already know what he did—don't you detective?"

Detective Franklin shot a glance over to Gwen as she came up to stand closer to him.

"Seems he followed his buddy out here, and you had gotten him a job working as an onsite cop at some private all girls' high school. Got fired though—seems he was a bit of a creeper, liked to walk the halls outside of the gym locker room—a little too often. Lots of complaints from the girls about his watching them all the time. Stinson told me he'd gotten him a job working nights at some parking garage—rent-a-cop security or something. I found him asleep in the booth when he was supposed to be walking the levels. I banged on the glass—told him someone had broken into my car, made him come out of the booth. That's when I got him. Easy-peasy."

"Rachel... thank you," Gwen said, moving to stand right next to the detective

"Thank you—for what?" Rachel turn her gaze to Gwen.

"For keeping my mother and me safe all these years."

"You know, none of them believe me," Rachel said to Gwen. "They all have to pay, like my father should have. No one was safe with them in this world. And this one here," she tightened the belt again and the old man gasped. "He's the last." Rachel lifted the taser to the old man's neck.

"Rachel, *please*... stop," Detective Franklin said. "Don't you recognize me?" He slowly lowered his gun.

"Jamie?" Rachel blinked, then shook her head rapidly back and forth.

"Yes... it's me, *Jamie*. Where did you go? I searched for you all night," the detective said, as if following Gwen's lead.

"I had to run...," Rachel began.

"Why did you leave me?" the detective asked, reaching out with words for the damaged girl he had once known. "I confronted your father that night, but he was drunk. He tried to run me off the road, but instead of him knocking me off my motorbike, he ran his car off the road and into the river. I think the impact killed him, or he drowned or both."

Rachel loosened her grip slightly on the belt, the taser still inches from the old man's throat.

"It was his fault—not mine, not yours," The detective said.

"I didn't know any of this—you don't understand... I... it broke my heart to leave you," Rachel said, desperate, almost as if her heart was breaking again now.

"We have a daughter," Jamie said, slicing a glance to Gwen then back to Rachel.

"You have a daughter. She's not *my* daughter—she belongs to Laura."

"I don't know Laura, I only know you," he said, taking a step closer and putting his gun back in his holster. He had his other hand outstretched towards her.

"Don't come any closer, Jamie. He has to pay," Rachel said, tightening the belt again.

"He didn't believe you—but I did. I know what your father did to you—all of it. I read your letters."

"My letters... *yes*. I was a good daughter—obedient, and still my father hurt me... and my mother abandoned me."

"She was weak... and you are strong," Detective Franklin said.

"She needed to pay for what she did to me. He needs to pay too."

The detective took another step forward. "Too many people have died—have paid for the sins of your father."

"They all deserve to die for what happened to me," she cried out. Tears began to well in her eyes now.

"Bad people deserve to be punished—I agree, but you should not have to do it. Look at my father," the detective said, glancing at his father. "He is an old man now—he suffers in his mind. Doesn't know what year it is—doesn't even know his own son."

"He was a horrible father to you," she sobbed.

"Yes, he was, but I'm not like him. I didn't become my father."

"Mom," Gwen said then. Rachel turned and looked at her. "Mom—*Rachel*, please let Laura be free of all of this."

"Rachel—you have become *that* which you had sought to destroy," Detective Franklin said as Gwen took a step past him.

"But I... they had to pay... I... don't you understand how my heart breaks... for you?" Rachel loosened the belt then, and dropped the taser, as she came to stand in front of the chair.

Detective Franklin crossed the distance to his father pulling Rachel away from him, as Gwen rushed forward to remove the belt from around the neck of the feeble and now seriously confused retired police chief.

Rachel leaned head-down into Jamie, limp in his arms. Tilting her head up then, she whispered in his ear, "*I am sorry.*" Then she grabbed the gun from his holster.

A single shot rang out through the room.

Epilog

September 20th, 2019

The University of Michigan Adult Inpatient Psychiatry Program
Case Study by: Dr. Marlene Branden
Patient: Rachel Rampton, A.k.a Laura Jameson, née Rampton
Case Notes:
Rachel Rampton survived a self-inflicted gunshot wound and was further deemed mentally incompetent to stand trial and sent to this mental health hospital within the unit for the criminally insane, where she now resides. No charges have been laid in the case of the murders committed by the serial killer known as The Small-Town Strangler, nor for the more recent murders of Professor Timothy Armstrong, the patient's mother Muriel Rampton, and officers Stinson and Thompson. Retired Police Chief James Franklin (senior) sustained only minor injuries and remains in the care of the private retirement center for seniors with Alzheimer's.

Based on my initial assessment, following the incident of her arrest, it appeared as though the patient at the time of the incident, had taken down the mental barrier between herself, Rachel, and that of her *alter*, Laura, and had shared her true memories, revealing to Laura her real past, showing her what had happened to her as a child and as a teenager, and sharing the truths about Jamie and Gwen and what she had done to protect them. I believe this to be the reason behind what had prompted the desire for her to attempt to commit suicide using Detective Franklin's gun.

When I first met with Rachel, I had asked her if she remembered what age she had been when *Laura had arrived*.

She couldn't recall, though she did tell me that she had chosen the name Laura. She had allowed Laura to believe her mother had given it to her and that it had been based on the name of a character in one of her mother's favorite television shows. Rachel had never been allowed to watch TV, but she often heard her mother swearing at the TV show, and commenting about how this Laura character was so well loved by the fans, but her mother hated this character for that very reason, and it was in fact, the reasons Rachel had chosen it. She had added that she'd not had a single friend growing up, there had been no birthday parties, no sleep overs, nothing of the sort, and it had been her mother's and ultimately her father's idea to keep control over her.

The next inquiry had been about the day Rachel had chosen to run away.

Rachel had told me that she'd left with only the clothes on her back and the ones she had backed in her knapsack. She said eventually had to *ditch* Jamie's motorcycle jacket, which she said had crushed her. But when she changed her name, she had chosen Jamison, in honor of him, the only man who had ever been kind to her. She had money from her job at the library and had used it to get away. During her time at the library, it was then that she had used the library's law books to find out how one went about changing their name. It wasn't that she hated Rachel, it was more that she had hated to hear her mother yell it, the way she had said it when she'd been mad at her. Rachel had been the name her father had picked, her mother had told her, and she had liked the name until her husband had told her why he had liked it. Apparently, she was named after Rachel Ward, an actress who had played a character in a movie about a woman who had fallen in love with a priest. Rachel had told me, that her mother was always jealous of other women, even of her own daughter.

Rachel had also told me that her mother hated her hair, and she worn it wild on purpose. She had had Laura lighten her hair to a strawberry blond similar to her daughter's hair, but then had changed it back when she had chosen not to use her disguise anymore, because she wanted the police chief to recognize her when she came to kill him. Rachel had said it had been a huge disappointment for she when she had found he had lost most of his faculties and why she hadn't killed him immediately. She had hoped he would eventually recognize her.

When asked about the birth of the patient's daughter Gwendolyn, I had received different accounts depending on which personality I had been speaking with at the time.

Laura had referred to it as the gift she received a week after her own birthday. She had been truly happy and had taken a photo of her and the baby with the hopes of sending it to her mother. She was optimistic that her mother would be missing her and that she would be kinder to her if she knew about the baby.

Rachel on the other hand, told a different story, where she called her mother with the intent of telling her how well she was doing and that she didn't need her or her father anymore. But on the call, her mother had cursed her name, had said her father was dead and it had been all Rachel's fault, that he died while he had been out looking for her. Her mother had told her she had always been an ungrateful selfish daughter and considered her a *whore* with regards to the relationship Rachel had had with her father, and that this baby only solidified her convictions.

It is my belief that the unexpected news of the patient's father's death and the further verbal abuse from the mother was what potentially caused the psychotic break and further fed Rachel's need to kill.

It had been Rachel's statement that, she had been killing her father over and over in the murders of these professor. Rachel considered herself the abused side and Laura as the free side. Rachel had explained to me that Laura was subconsciously driven by her and without her knowledge, that she had started to write letters to her mother about the killings, and the killings had been the driving force behind moving poor Laura from town to town. She'd had Laura convinced she was being tracked by the man Rachel had set in her mind, had raped her, and was now killing for her. That was how she was to keep them safe. As Rachel's letter to Gwen had stated, she kept Laura scared to keep her from going to the police.

The next subject had been about Laura going home to see her ailing mother.

Rachel told me that after the death of her father, her mother had remained in the house collecting his pension and insurance from the college. When she went there, she had found that her mother had kept her letters in her father's office, only the first of them opened and read, so she had taken them, along with her father's belt, the one he used to restrain her with when he'd molested her and then later used to beat her. She told me that she killed her mother, that I already knew, but she had also stated that for them to truly be free, for *her* to truly be free, she had needed to get rid of all those who had harmed her. Her father was already dead, so it meant she'd need only kill those two police officers, the ones who *hadn't* helped her, and that police chief who had been so cruel to her and had been so dismissive to his son Jamie.

On my previous visit with the patient, I had addressed the question from Detective Franklin, though it had been mainly a curiosity of his regarding the murder of Officer Stinson in his laneway, and how Rachel had gotten out there and past the guard at the gated community.

Rachel had said it had been a tricky one with the gate, but the map on her phone had shown the house had been near a golf course. So, she had instructed the taxi driver to take her there, to the golf course in lieu of the house. There had been no security at the entrance, and she'd cut across the property and through the woods that came out close to the end of the block the house had been on. It was just a short distance to the house from there and it had still been dark out. She had cut along the back of the fences after, to keep out of sight, since there had been a shot gun blast and all. She said she had gotten *super lucky* when she had found him in his driveway. If she had been a few minutes later, she would have found him dead already, *but what fun would that have been?* she had stated.

During my sessions with the patient, I have found that when I am speaking with Laura, she prefers the analytical part of our sessions, and chats with me as if we were colleagues discussing a patient, though still similar in dialog to that of our original friendship.

Whereas Rachel prefers to try to shock and awe me with what her father did to her, with what she did to those men and why. She likes to ask me if I know why she did it, and if I think she liked it. Laura does the same but from the view of a physician treating a patient. She doesn't like when I bring up Gwen or Jamie, and I have yet to find out why she won't speak of her daughter. Rachel on the other hand, likes to ask how Jamie is doing and often tells me how he was her first. I don't know if that is the truth, about him being her first, but something in her expression when she talks about him leads me to believe he was. This is the only time Rachel speaks sweetly, in the remembering of Jamie.

Though I have had numerous dialogs with both Rachel and Laura, I am reluctant to say who is the dominant personality now. Originally I had thought Rachel to be the dominant, but with further examination, I have found that since Laura had been the one who had worked and raised a child, who had done all the moving and was the personality shown most to the world, it became apparent to me that Laura behaved as the grownup while Rachel was the reckless one. Though it was Rachel who thought she had been taking care of Laura all these years, protecting her. Laura was the stable one, the steady and consistent personality. It hadn't been until Laura had seen that professor at Gwen's school bothering the female students, that Rachel's personality had surfaced again.

I wonder now if perhaps they have merged, or if they now share dominants. When we meet at our scheduled time, I never know who I am initially going to be speaking with nor for how long. Upon entering the patient's room, if I am in the presence of Rachel, she normally has her long wavy hair down and she is always standing to greet me, and her mood with me is usually rebellious, and very clever and ambitious.

If it is Laura waiting for me when I enter the room, she is always seated, with her hair pulled back and tidy. Her mood is typically much more conservative, timid but likeable, and she exudes the personality I am most familiar with, that of a smart, hardworking people pleaser.

They are both clever, they both like to give me the impression they are the smarter of the two, even smarter than myself. They even sometimes like to try to trick me and pretend to be the other. Today, when I had entered the patient's room, she had been standing next to the set of chairs provided for our consultations. Her dark red hair had been loose and wild, and she had addressed me with, *"Hello, Dr. Branden,"* giving me the impression I would be conversing with Rachel, but then the patient had sat down, and she'd secured her wild red hair back into a bun. Then she changed her greeting to, *"Hey you—I was so excited to hear you were coming to see me today,"* and delivered in a manner familiar to me as Laura's.

This game, this switching of identities has had me wondering if Rachel's mind had ever really split, or was it they—or just Rachel, who was playing a sort of game with everyone, all along. The one thing I know for certain, beyond all other doubts, is that she—they, will never get to leave this place.

* * *

THE END

Made in the USA
Columbia, SC
20 February 2021